A DEATH FORETOLD

As he crept inside the barn, Touch the Sky's eyes cut to a few wooden rungs that had been nailed into a support beam, making a crude ladder up into a hayloft.

He should secure the loft, he realized. But it was more logical to look around down here first. Anyone hiding in the loft would be bound to make noise coming down. Touch the Sky was safe from surprise attack, so long as he didn't offer a clear target.

Hugging the wall, crawling on his knees and elbows, Touch the Sky moved cautiously down to the pile of dirt, eased around it, and abruptly felt a cold stirring in his stomach.

A tunnel entrance yawned before him, a hungry maw calling out to him to enter if he dared.

Why should this bother you? he admonished himself. After all, you knew it was here. You heard Carlson mention it. So why this feeling now as if a dead man had risen before your eyes?

You know perfectly well why that feeling, another voice inside him responded. Because you saw this tunnel long before Carlson mentioned it. You saw it in your dream vision.

Death by water...

Blood on the Arrows

CHEYENNE

RIVER OF
DEATH

JUDD COLE

LEISURE BOOKS   **NEW YORK CITY**

A LEISURE BOOK®

March 1997

Published by

Dorchester Publishing Co., Inc.
276 Fifth Avenue
New York, NY 10001

Printed in the United States of America.

RIVER OF DEATH

Prologue

Although Matthew Hanchon bore the name given to him by his adopted white parents, he was the son of full-blooded Northern Cheyennes. The lone survivor of a Bluecoat massacre in 1840, the infant was raised by John and Sarah Hanchon in the Wyoming Territory settlement of Bighorn Falls.

His adoptive parents loved him as their own, and at first the youth was happy enough in his limited world. The occasional stares and threats from others meant little—until his sixteenth year and a forbidden love with Kristen, daughter of wealthy rancher Hiram Steele.

Steele's campaign to run Matthew off like a distempered wolf was assisted by Seth Carlson, the jealous, Indian-hating cavalry officer who was in love with Kristen. Carlson delivered a fateful ultimatum: Either Matthew cleared out of Bighorn Falls for good, or Carlson would ruin his parents' contract to supply nearby Fort Bates—and thus ruin their mercantile business.

His heart sad but determined, Matthew set out for the upcountry of the Powder River, Cheyenne territory. Captured by braves from Chief Yellow Bear's tribe, he was declared an Indian spy for the hair-face soldiers and brutally tortured over fire. But only a heartbeat before he was to be scalped and gutted, old Arrow Keeper interceded.

The tribe shaman and protector of the sacred Medicine Arrows, Arrow Keeper had recently experienced an epic vision. This vision foretold that the long-lost son of a great Cheyenne chief would return to his people—and that he would lead them in one last, great victory against their enemies. This youth would be known by the distinctive mark of the warrior, the same birthmark Arrow Keeper spotted buried past this youth's hairline: a mulberry-colored arrowhead.

Arrow Keeper used his influence to spare the youth's life, and ordered that he be allowed to join the tribe and train with the junior warriors. This infuriated two braves especially: the fierce war leader Black Elk and his cunning younger cousin, Wolf Who Hunts Smiling.

Black Elk was jealous of the glances cast at the tall young stranger by Honey Eater, daughter of Chief Yellow Bear. And Wolf Who Hunts Smiling, proudly ambitious despite his youth, hated all whites without exception. This stranger was to him only a make-believe Cheyenne who wore white man's shoes, spoke the paleface tongue, and showed his emotions in his face like the woman-hearted white men.

Arrow Keeper buried the youth's white name forever and gave him a new Cheyenne name: Touch the Sky. But he remained a white man's dog in the eyes of many in the tribe. At first humiliated at every turn, eventually the determined youth mastered the warrior arts. Slowly, as his coup stick filled with enemy scalps, he won the respect of more and more in the tribe.

But with each victory, deceiving appearances triumphed over reality, and the acceptance he so desperately craved eluded him. Worse, his hard-won victories left him with two especially fierce enemies outside the tribe: a Blackfoot called Sis-ki-dee and a Comanche named Big Tree.

As for Black Elk, at first he was hard but fair. When Touch the Sky rode off to save his white parents from outlaws, Honey Eater was convinced that he had deserted her and the tribe forever. She was forced to accept Black Elk's bride-price after her father crossed to the Land of Ghosts. But Touch the Sky returned.

Then, as it became clear to all that Honey Eater loved only Touch the Sky, Black Elk's jealousy drove him to join his younger cousin in plotting against Touch the Sky's life. Finally, Wolf Who Hunts Smiling's treachery forced a crisis: Aiming at Touch the Sky in heavy fog, he instead killed Black Elk. Touch the Sky stood accused of the murder by many in the tribe.

Judd Cole

Though it divided the tribe irrevocably, he and Honey Eater performed the squaw-taking ceremony. He had firm allies in his blood brother Little Horse, the youth Two Twists, and Tangle Hair. With Arrow Keeper's mysterious disappearance, Touch the Sky became the tribe's shaman.

But a pretend shaman named Medicine Flute, backed by Touch the Sky's enemies, challenged his authority. And despite his fervent need to stop being the eternal outsider, Touch the Sky was still trapped between two worlds, welcome in neither.

Chapter One

"Tell us a thing, shaman, if you are so wise,"
Little Horse taunted his tall friend. "For I have
noticed something curious."

Little Horse had to speak loudly to be heard
above the foaming of the rapids further out in
the river. He, Two Twists, and Tangle Hair sat
in a little group, watching Touch the Sky's son
receive his first swimming lesson. Little Bear,
his second winter just behind him, dangled naked between Touch the Sky and Honey Eater.
Clearly the river both intrigued and frightened
him. His parents held him in up to his navel,
and he was still deciding whether to laugh or
cry.

"Let *me* tell you a thing, All Behind Him," replied Two Twists, youngest of the Cheyenne
braves present. He used the name he had given

Little Horse when the latter began to gain weight. "Here is something very curious. They say a good warrior takes on the traits of his enemies. This Not-So-Little Horse here—he must be a good warrior indeed. See? He is getting a belly pouch like the beer-swilling paleface soldiers."

"Soon," Tangle Hair added, watching the little one decide to laugh with delight, "Little Horse will take to eating beef and mounting his pony from the white man's side."

Even Honey Eater, busy restraining her squirming charge, smiled at the teasing behind them. Usually the braves acted so solemn and taciturn when women and children were around. But this trio, as close as brothers to Touch the Sky, accepted her and the child as trusted equals and let their guards down. Great warriors, she had learned, were often like adolescent boys when among their own. But there were no boys among this group when the war cry sounded.

Little Horse, grinning with the rest, threatened to flay Two Twists' soles. A moment later the two braves were struggling in a wrestling contest, grunting and cursing.

"A new buck knife on Little Horse," Touch the Sky said automatically, for no Indian passed a chance to wager.

Tangle Hair nodded. "A double pipe of white man's tobacco on Two Twists."

"Treachery!" Two Twists shouted in a muffled voice. "The big Indian is sitting on me! Have you seen how swayback all his ponies have become? I am defeated! Take my hair and let me breathe!"

Touch the Sky laughed outright at his companions as he dipped his son even lower, letting the cool mountain runoff rise up under the mite's armpits.

"Brrrr!" Little Bear roared, imitating his mother on a winter morning. His impressive lung power had earned him his name.

This made all of them laugh again. Little Horse and Two Twists quit struggling long enough to admire the little warrior as he dipped his head quickly under the water with no help from either parent.

"Ipewa," Little Horse said, nodding his approval. "Good! Just as the line-back dun always breeds good stock, this Touch the Sky has given our tribe a fighter! Look at him! The entire world knows we Shayienas are not fish-eaters or great swimmers. I have watched good Cheyenne babes of four and five cry in the river. This little tadpole wants to swim right in."

Touch the Sky nodded proudly, though in fact his companions were almost as pleased as he. There was no word for "orphan" in Cheyenne, because every adult was considered a parent to every child. And Touch the Sky had already assured his companions that Little Bear would not exist if not for their vigilance and loyalty in protecting mother and son.

"He wants to wade right in," Touch the Sky agreed. "But he must learn what Arrow Keeper taught me. Search the water first."

Even as he said this, Touch the Sky scooped

Judd Cole

one hand into the purling river, just ahead of his floundering son. It emerged holding a jagged-edged object made of metal torn to lethally sharp points and edges. The child had been about to flounder onto it.

Everyone, Little Bear and Honey Eater included, stared at it.

"What in the name of Maiyun is it?" Honey Eater demanded.

The trio on the bank behind them were not as mystified as Honey Eater was. Because any companion of Touch the Sky's was, by necessity, a veteran warrior, they had a better idea what the object was. They were more worried about why it was there.

"It is a shell casing," Touch the Sky replied, now ignoring his son to search the low, rolling banks around them and the scattered clumps of cottonwood. They had picked a secluded spot well upriver from their summer camp. "A shell that has been exploded further upriver and washed down."

He looked at Little Horse. "Buck, you were about to ask me a thing when double-braid here started teasing you. Let me ask that question for you. You are curious about the same thing troubling many of us. The river. We are well into the snowmelt moon, and the freshets have been plentiful. With so much runoff from the mountains, you wonder, why are the Powder and Little Powder Rivers down this season?"

Little Horse stood up, watching Touch the Sky with open admiration.

"Once again, shaman, you have seen with the

14

inner eye. That is the very thing I wonder. Does this"—he nodded toward the twisted scrap in his friend's hand—"somehow explain it?"

Slowly, with Little Bear kicking in spirited protest, Touch the Sky lifted his son and carried him out of the river. Honey Eater followed, her soft doeskin dress wet and clinging to her long legs and the deep, sweeping curves of her hips. Fresh white columbine petals were braided through her hair.

"Explain it?" Touch the Sky repeated, handing the child to Two Twists for a ride on his shoulders. "If so, I do not know how. But these casings are not from explosives used by combat soldiers. They are engineering charges."

Touch the Sky had been forced to use crude Cheyenne equivalents for the paleface words, just as artillery pieces were called big-talking guns. His companions listened to him, but still looked baffled.

"When I grew up among the whites near Fort Bates," Touch the Sky explained, "the soldiers used explosives to level ridges and build bridges or to clear out rocky areas. Engineering charges."

"Like the ones Wolf Who Hunts Smiling and the renegades stole from the blue blouses?" Two Twists asked. "The explosives they used to destroy the path for the iron horse?"

Touch the Sky nodded.

"Brothers, all well and good," Tangle Hair said. "But what do blue flowers have to do with the causes of the wind? Look. See there where the watermark is? Far lower than it should be this time of the season. Where will it be by the time we enter the dry moons? Surely this is bad medicine, not the work of palefaces or Indian renegades with explosives."

This sounded reasonable to each of the Cheyennes, for in their world natural causes took far greater precedence over man-made ones. If the red-speckled cough wiped out your village, it was the work of angry Holy Ones, not an infected blanket.

Touch the Sky respected those natural causes, but his time among whites also taught him respect for man's power to disturb and control nature.

"It is bad medicine," he replied, "no matter the cause. But we have wasted enough words in useless speculation."

He turned to Honey Eater. "Take the little one back to camp. Two Twists and Tangle Hair will ride with you. Little Horse and I are taking a ride upriver to see what can be seen."

No one questioned this, although a troubled light glinted briefly in Honey Eater's eyes. When the rest had left, Touch the Sky and Little Horse caught up their ponies.

"I knew your question before you asked it," Touch the Sky said, "because an omen was placed over my eyes last night in a dream."

"What omen, brother?"

Touch the Sky always tried to be forthright with his band, especially with Little Horse. How many times had they stood back-to-back and cheated death? But this particular omen was so forboding and ominous that speaking of it directly might create powerful bad medicine.

"An omen," the tall warrior replied, swinging up onto his little paint, "that augured trouble by water."

Little Horse was not a brave to show feelings in his face. But this statement, from this highly credible source, shook him to his core. He could read beneath the words. His friend had seen an omen promising death in the water—the worst possible way in the world for an Indian to die. A drowned Indian could never go to the Land of Ghosts. His spirit remained trapped in the water for eternity, cold and lonely, moaning in grief but completely without succor.

Better the bullet, the arrow, the lance, even the deadly Comanche skull-cracker than death in the water.

And because it was bad this time, Little Horse grinned wide and mustered his famous bravado.

"Go forth and bring me the Wendigo," he boasted. "I have no plans to die in my tipi."

Touch the Sky grinned. "Unlike the skinny Medicine Flute, who boasts he can divine the future, I have no foreknowledge of events. But I can tell you this, buck. You will never die in your tipi. Not," he added regretfully, "so long as you cross your lance with mine. Now look sharp, brother. We are about to grab trouble firmly by the tail."

One full sleep's ride west of the Cheyenne camp, in the center of the verdant bottom section white men called Blackford's Valley, an

17

odd coalition had assembled inside a sagging hay barn.

A huge, heavy-jowled man with thick lumps of scar tissue over his eyes spoke to the rest from his perch atop a stack of shoring timbers.

"Men!" shouted Hiram Steele. "It's already starting to rain gold! I called you all together today to make an announcement. Thanks to your efforts so far, I've been able to impress some extremely solvent investors in my Pikestown project. Your wages are guaranteed for the next six months!"

A rousing cheer went up from the twenty men gathered around Hiram. They were all soldiers, though most had removed their blue kersey blouses and were either bare-chested or wore only coarse gray linen undershirts.

Steele lifted a hand to quiet the men.

"Now understand, men. These investors don't know about our little operation here at Salt Lick Creek. I'm keeping it dark from them just the way that you men and Captain Carlson are keeping it dark from your superiors back at Fort Bates."

Hiram had provided a barrel of good grain mash for this occasion. An anonymous trooper, his tongue well oiled with coffin varnish, piped up:

"You ride for Cap'n Carlson, mum's the word! A high private can live like a general in Savvy Seth's platoon! Who *wouldn't* be a soldier!"

Carlson, the only officer in the group and standing closest to Hiram, scowled. "Sew up your lips, Meadows," he growled while the rest of the troopers laughed.

Hiram watched Carlson scowl and forced back a good chuckle. Carlson was crooked as a sidewinder, which made him one of Hiram's most useful business partners here on the frontier. But the West Point graduate and scion of one of the First Families of Virginia had never learned to relax around common men. His men liked serving under him because they could often triple their regular pay by carrying out his and Hiram's schemes. But they had no real respect for him, a fact Carlson was smart enough to grasp but too bullheaded to change.

"Men," Hiram continued, "Pikestown will become a reality, I'm sure of that. Our operation is perfectly brilliant in its simplicity. This barn—" He swept one beefy arm overhead, indicating the building. Behind the knot of men, huge piles of dirt obscured a tunnel opening. "—keeps our operation secret. The initial blasting is almost over and gave us a good operating base. Now the digging makes the change so gradual no one suspects any cause but Mother Nature. Soon Salt Lick Creek is going to undergo one of those 'natural' changes that happen all the time. It's going to shift its course to an old tributary. And once that happens, it means far less water downstream for the blanket-asses living at the Cheyenne camp. Meantime, it also means irrigation water for my— our—projected farming community."

Hiram didn't bother adding a technicality that didn't concern Carlson's work crew. Salt Lick Creek was the official treaty boundary of the Northern Cheyenne reservation. Once it jumped its bank to a new tributary, it would cut the reservation in half. Meanwhile, the value of Hiram's new claim at the land office in Register Cliffs was about to increase dramatically. Land now wasted on buffalo range would provide the fertile bottomland for his new community of Pikestown.

All it took was one bend in one good-sized creek. And that bend was being created from underground, using trained military sappers, and by scraping-and-grading crews working after dark.

While the sappers debauched, Hiram got Carlson aside.

"Did your C.O. buy that story about building a cistern near Beaver Creek?"

"Sure," Carlson said. "It's his favorite project. He loves it when the paper-collar boys from the press quote him on how the Army is giving back to the American people."

"You've got a few of your boys working on it?"

Carlson nodded. He was a big, bluff man with wind-blistered cheeks. He still wore his cavalry officer's hat, the brim snapped back to keep his vision clear.

"A small crew. Luckily for us, Colonel Nearhood doesn't know his ass from his elbow when it comes to engineering. He thinks building a rain cistern is a major job. He doesn't realize this is too many men in the field."

Carlson seemed to be listening, but Hiram could tell his mind was somewhere else. And he knew right where it was.

"You're fretting about Hanchon, ain't you?" he said.

Carlson nodded again. "You telling me you're not?"

Hiram frowned. "You think I'd lie to you after all that red bastard's done to us? Man, my own daughter was sweet on that sonofabitch! I caught him up in her bedroom before that whore got wise and ran away from home. I swear it now, I mean to kill him *and* Kristen."

Carlson flushed red to his very earlobes. "You're telling *me* about being shamed by that red nigger and Kristen? Me, who asked her to marry me, only to find out she preferred a flea-bitten, blanket-assed savage over a decent white man?"

"Never mind the shame, soldier blue. Think about the money. We've both put our last red cent into this project. If it works, we're going to die rich with counties named after us. And it *should* work. The brilliance is that all of our work is secret. I can tell you right now, Hanchon *will* be coming, and soon, to check this out. That gives us a chance to kill him. It's also an opportunity to see just how secret our operation is."

Carlson nodded, his features set tight with determination. "He'll be coming. He always does. But we've never been ready for him like we are now. This time, he's riding into a world of hurt."

Chapter Two

"Count upon it," Touch the Sky told his companion. "Back at camp they are celebrating in the Bull Whip dance lodge."

Little Horse nodded. "Celebrating? Brother, they will paint as for war and hold a victory dance! Every time you ride out, they gloat. Your enemies leap atop the stumps and scream: 'See? See how it is? Once again this Touch the Sky rides out without benefit of council! He has gone to play the dog for his hair-face masters!' "

Touch the Sky laughed so hard that he had to slow his pony to a walk. For Little Horse had done an excellent imitation of the whiny-voiced Medicine Flute, pretender to the title of tribal shaman.

The two warriors had ridden perhaps a half sleep's ride up the winding course of the Powder, in no hurry except when exposed too long without cover. Both braves had kept talk to a minimum—this mystery of the receding water level required careful observation to solve it, not endless and pointless discussion.

But now it was time to share a few thoughts. Touch the Sky dropped the paint's buffalo-hair reins, letting them dangle over the horse's ears. Automatically the well-trained pony slowed to a walk, grazing at will on the lush spring bunchgrass covering the river flat.

"The water is down for the entire length," Touch the Sky said.

"As you say." Little Horse produced his clay pipe from a legging sash. He stuffed it with willow-bark tobacco and the two braves smoked to the four directions.

"The water is down," Little Horse repeated, "and going down still more. Look. See that exposed wall of shale there? See the marks? Like rings on a tree. They show each day's level. Brother," Little Horse added, his voice showing concern, "this is no little event. Our tribe is in trouble."

Touch the Sky nodded, his lips pressed in a tight, straight line as they always were when he was baffled or concerned.

"Not little," he agreed. "And if that shell casing we found means anything, we know palefaces are involved. Tell me a thing. What else do we know?"

His stout friend met his eye, face impassive. "We know," Little Horse suggested, "that a certain rider left camp soon after we did. But he did not follow us. He merely determined our direction. Then he rode wide to our flank and sped on ahead."

Touch the Sky nodded at all this, well satisfied. Little Horse could find sign where other men saw only bare rock. The dust puffs, appearing soon after they passed their camp, had been faint as wisps of smoke. But both braves had spotted them. Then Touch the Sky had climbed a tree to look.

"A certain rider," Touch the Sky agreed now, "on a pure black pony flying the Bull Whip streamer from its tail. Now tell me another thing. Why did this rider not follow us?"

"Because he knows where we are going. Or better, he knows what we are doing, that we are looking for some cause for this odd trouble with the river."

"As you say." Touch the Sky's eyes slitted against the bright sunlight as they scanned the vast country surrounding them. "And knowing that, where has he gone?"

Little Horse enjoyed this game thoroughly, though his face showed nothing.

"Where else? To warn whoever else he is scheming with that we are coming."

"Better and better," Touch the Sky said. "We have cracked the shell. Now let us expose the meat. Since that rider on the black pony is Wolf Who Hunts Smiling, who is he going to warn?"

"Probably Sis-ki-dee and Big Tree," Little Horse speculated. "Among others. Those three jays are always together for mischief though the Wolf is clever at denying it."

"Those two, certainly," Touch the Sky said. "But the explosives hint that he is also honeying up to his white partners. Hiram Steele is back, brother, all signs point to it. And if Steele comes to the lick, Seth Carlson will come with him."

This talk made both braves a little nervous. Big Tree, Sis-ki-dee, Hiram Steele, Seth Carlson, Wolf Who Hunts Smiling—it was a roster of their most deadly enemies. Any one of them alone could give ten men grief. Together, no man's hell could corral them.

Now Little Horse, too, scanned the surrounding terrain. From long experience, both friends watched for the places that gave marksmen a good bead. They avoided stopping for more than a few seconds. When on the move, they automatically picked up and slowed the pace in the open, making it difficult for a distant rifleman to "lead" them.

"In matters of speculation, shaman," Little Horse said, "you are wrong about as often as the Yellow River runs clear. So Steele is back with a new scheme to make the red man's life a hurting place. What can it be? What is he doing to our river?"

"Ask me where the sun sleeps, while you are at it. That's why we are riding, buck. To see what we can see. For now, know this. Our enemies have no plans to make our mission easy for us. And thanks to Wolf Who Hunts Smiling, they will know we are coming. Is today a good day to die?" Touch the Sky demanded.

Little Horse grinned, sliding his revolving four-barreled scattergun from its rope rigging.

"Not today," he replied. "Today it's one bullet for one enemy!"

"Cheyenne People!" shouted Medicine Flute. "Do you see how it is? Our river is drying up! And now this tall one who once wore white man's shoes has again mysteriously ridden out. He has ridden—"

"—out without benefit of council!" Tangle Hair finished for him. He shouted from a group of Bow String soldiers loyal to Touch the Sky and the tribe's new peace chief, River of Winds. "You sing a familiar litany, bone-blower! And you only sing it when Touch the Sky is gone."

Medicine Flute flushed with rage at the words "bone-blower." This was a reference to his flute, made from the leg bone of a dead Pawnee. He played it constantly, claiming its notes could influence the High Holy Ones. All anyone could verify, however, was that hearing it made infants squall.

"As you say," Medicine Flute said coldly. "I use your own words back on you: 'when Touch the Sky is gone.' I am only suggesting, as shaman, what the average brave has noticed: Touch the Sky only seems to be gone when serious trouble besets this tribe."

"As shaman?" Tangle Hair demanded. He was on his own now, for Two Twists would not leave the site of Touch the Sky's tipi—not with Honey Eater and Little Bear inside, unprotected in this hostile village. "You? Shaman? Not in *this* world, brave imposter. Put all your 'medicine'

26

in an empty parfleche, and you'll have an empty parfleche."

A few of the Bow Strings laughed, supporting Tangle Hair. But a few others were nervous. They trusted Touch the Sky well enough. But this Medicine Flute had often impressed them with his apparent magic. And after all, it was common knowledge that men other than official shamen could possess medicine.

"Brave talk," Medicine Flute responded, "means little once the worm has turned. It matters little who has the official title of shaman. All that matters is the doing. And you may speak up for your leader all you wish. You cannot alter facts. Once again he is gone!"

Medicine Flute had no official right to gather the people in the clearing. But "official" meant little in this tribe divided against itself. For his own safety, Chief River of Winds made very few appearances outside of the regular council meetings. His respect for Touch the Sky, steadfastly maintained even when appearances damned the tall brave, made him a prime target for Touch the Sky's numerous enemies.

"Yes, Touch the Sky is gone," Tangle Hair shouted so all could hear, even those huddled in lodges and tipis. "Any time he seeks to help his people, he must go alone. In the past, every attempt to work through the Council of Forty was thwarted. We all know a burned baby fears the fire. Why should Touch the Sky keep addressing the headmen when they are grouped against him? Never mind Touch the Sky. Wolf Who Hunts Smiling, too, is gone. Neither did *he* seek permission of council. And who will wager that he went out to pick new flowers?"

"I've learned my lesson with Matthew Hanchon," Hiram Steele told the rest of them. "There was a time when I consigned the bastard to the grave without taking his measure. Now I've taken it, and each time I hold up the rule, he's growed. I'll never say that red son is dead until I hold his heart in my hand."

Sis-ki-dee, who knew some English, threw back his close-cropped head and roared with crazy laughter.

"*Hold* his heart?" the renegade Blackfoot warrior scoffed. "I mean to eat it! But you speak straight-arrow when you warn us not to dance yet. That one sheds death like a snake sheds skins."

They huddled in a council circle inside the dilapidated old hay barn: Hiram, Sis-ki-dee, the Comanche terror Big Tree, and Wolf Who Hunts Smiling. Seth Carlson was down in the tunnel under Salt Lick Creek, inspecting progress on the operation to shift the creek's flow. Wolf Who Hunts Smiling had just arrived from his Cheyenne camp with news that the brave he called Woman Face was finally riding their way.

Big Tree, built more like a Mescalero Apache than a Comanche, made a barking sound of contempt. Like most Comanches from the Blanco Canyon country, he was fluent in Spanish and proficient in English. He leveled a sneering gaze on Sis-ki-dee.

"This one speaks with new respect since his

clash with the tall one up in Bloody Bones Canyon."

Sis-ki-dee was not one to show consternation. But this remark made him stare at the ground. Hot shame seeped into his face.

Wolf Who Hunts Smiling only snorted and looked away, for he, too, knew the story well by now. But Hiram was newly returned to the territory.

"What happened up in Bloody Bones Canyon?" he demanded.

Big Tree started to reply—started to say something about how the mighty Sis-ki-dee, known as the Red Peril throughout the Bear Paw country, had actually begged Touch the Sky to spare his life. But the sudden, murderous glint in the Blackfoot warrior's eyes silenced him.

"The same thing happened to me," Sis-ki-dee said stiffly, "that has happened to every man here, more than once. The tall one defeated me."

"You've put the ax right on the haft," Hiram said approvingly. "That arrogant sonofabitch has given all of us a comeuppance. He's due. Way overdue. Any time now, he's going to ride within range of our mounted videttes. That's our first line of defense. Six sharpshooters, and whoever plugs Hanchon gets two thousand dollars in gold double eagles. That motivates a man to aim steady and squeeze slow."

Behind the little circle, sappers operated a hand winch to remove buckets of dirt and muck from below. So far it was being piled inside the barn to disguise the underground operation.

"After the videttes," Hiram continued, "come the sniper stations. Four of them, set up on bluffs overlooking the river. Seth handpicked these men and equipped them with bipods and long-distance Hawken rifles. Fifty-four caliber—the old buffalo ball. You hit a man *anywhere* on his body with that little puppy, he's carrion.

"But let's say our buck decides to defy Cheyenne tradition and move at night." Hiram nodded toward Sis-ki-dee and Big Tree. "Two of the best night fighters on the plains. You two may smell like a whorehouse at low tide, but I'd rather face a grizzly than either one of you after dark."

"Or before it," Big Tree added. Hiram—a big man himself—scowled at this, but said nothing to contradict it.

"Mounted videttes, snipers, you two," Hiram summed up. "But let's just pretend he slips past or through all of it. So what? Unless he gets inside this barn—which we can easily prevent—he will never even guess what the hell is going on. All you see above ground is a big, fast-flowing creek that's shifting its course for 'natural' reasons."

This made the three Indians stare back toward the tunnel. Hiram noticed the apprehensive look on all three faces and grinned. Not only did many red men fear being underwater, they hated even more a confined space—one like this tunnel under the river.

"Care to inspect the operation?" Hiram asked, goading them.

"Would *you* care to hang from your teats by metal hooks for an entire day in a broiling sun?" Wolf Who Hunts Smiling demanded. This was the standard initiation for young Sioux and Cheyenne warriors. "Hair-face," he added, "when you listed all the obstacles Woman Face must defeat, you left one out."

"Which?"

The cunning Cheyenne brave slid his obsidian knife from its sheath. He was small but wiry and strong, with the swift, furtive eyes of one who is constantly on guard for the ever-expected attack.

"You forgot me. Long before any of you vowed to send him over, I stepped between him and the campfire in front of witnesses. To a Cheyenne this is a vow that I mean to kill him. Until I fulfill that vow, I can never truly control the best braves."

Hiram nodded, liking the sound of this. "Plenty of good reasons to kill him. Don't forget, for all I know that filthy red—uhh, Hanchon topped my own daughter. He's also cost me a fortune and got my ass tossed into court. I don't care whose bullet kills him. I just know he needs killing."

Chapter Three

"What is it, shaman?" Little Horse demanded.

The two Cheyenne warriors had stopped and dropped their ponies' halters to let them drink from a backwater of the Powder River. This permitted them to shelter in the thickets rather than risk the open banks.

Touch the Sky had been in the act of peeling loose a sheet of pemmican from the roll in his parfleche, for the warriors had decided to build no cooking fires as they explored the river. Suddenly he looked up and stared toward the distant horizon as if he could hear music there.

But Little Horse, famed for the keenest ears in the tribe, heard nothing. "What?" he demanded again. "What did you hear?"

Touch the Sky shook his head. "It is a feeling, buck, not a noise."

"What manner of feeling? Shaman feelings?"

"Some call me shaman, but many have felt knowledge in their bones. It was a feeling any man might have. It is a warning. A reminder that a man can never be too ready."

Little Horse nodded, understanding. He thought they were being vigilant, but Touch the Sky was saying what must be said. They had faced down much danger in the past, had each come within a hairsbreadth of death more than once. The more a man survived, the more he began to delude himself that he was invincible. And once he believed that, he was worm fodder.

"The country is turning against us now," Touch the Sky said. "We are nearing the spot whites call Blackford's Valley."

"I call it Wendigo," Little Horse declared. "Once before we faced Carlson and Steele in that death trap. Brother, I would follow you into the white man's Hell carrying an empty quiver if you ordered it. But I do not think I would again stay in that stone lodge in Blackford's Valley."

This talk troubled Touch the Sky more than his friend realized. The stone lodge Little Horse meant was the abandoned mill where the Cheyennes had once been forced to take shelter from soldier patrols. Even the stout Little Horse had been reluctant to sleep under a roof; and he had positively quailed when forced to crawl through a short escape tunnel out of the mill.

Natural enough fears in an Indian, thought Touch the Sky. He had once watched a brave

Sioux warrior reduced to quivering fright when confronted with his first flight of stairs. The trouble was, if that omen Touch the Sky had experienced earlier had been correct, Little Horse might indeed have to once again face a confined space. A confined space that just might fill up with water . . .

"The valley offers excellent cover for an enemy," Touch the Sky continued. "Yet we must examine the river through that stretch. Especially the confluence where Salt Lick Creek feeds in. Much of the flow during the warm moons is from the creek. Perhaps there has merely been a huge sawyer formed, and it has turned into a natural dam. That happened once up on the Tongue, recall it? If so, we can bring men back and clear it."

For a few heartbeats Little Horse brightened at this prospect. Then he shook his head.

"Perhaps," he conceded. "But the warning you felt just now would not portend such luck. Time to ride, brother. And I mean to respect that feeling you had, shaman or no. For indeed, no man can be too careful."

Baylis Morningstar unsnapped the rawhide pouch on his sash and removed a pair of brass binoculars. Making sure they would not reflect a stray beam of sunlight, he began a careful study of the terrain where the Powder River entered Blackford's Valley.

The half-breed was a former Army scout who'd fled back to the wilds after killing a sergeant during a gambling match. Captain Seth

Carlson had contacted him by way of an Indian runner with this job offer. Baylis liked being a vidette, a mounted sentry. He got to work on his own. That was when he was at his most efficient. And after all, he thought, he had killed eighteen men over the years, each one on his own and without witnesses. Then the first time he'd killed a man with witnesses, he'd been forced to become a fugitive. From now on, he worked alone. Always.

He elevated and traversed with the binoculars, methodically studying every bit of the terrain. His dun stood well behind him, hobbled foreleg to rear. Baylis traveled light—his saddle was merely a sheepskin pad with a leather surcingle and brass stirrups. The entire rig weighed only three pounds. He had stolen it from a Papago Indian he'd killed down south on the Staked Plains of west Texas.

He halted the glasses for a long moment, studying a point just out from the east rim of the valley. In the thickets there, he had just seen a few birds fly up as if startled.

His lips twitched in a little smile. He knew all about this tall legend called Touch the Sky of the Northern Cheyenne. Cheyennes . . . no braves to fool with. Their enemies always referred to them as "the Fighting Cheyennes."

But he also knew the value of white man's gold. To most Indians on the Great Plains, it was still just a glittering yellow rock—good for decorating one's war vest or a squaw's shawl. But Baylis had spent time among the hair-face warriors. He knew how those pretty yellow coins were more valuable even than fine furs. They could be traded for fine coffee, good weapons and saddles, the best liquor. Whoever killed this Touch the Sky would never spend another hard winter.

Again Baylis patiently studied that spot where he had seen the birds scatter. He saw nothing else, but that didn't discourage him. These braves who would be coming—they were the best among the best. There would be few warnings.

While he studied the terrain, Baylis felt his stomach growl with hunger. He glanced quickly around. Down near the creek, a fat brown rabbit was nibbling some wild turnip leaves.

The half-breed laid his binoculars aside and slipped a slingshot from the pouch on his sash. It was small but powerfully constructed, carved from bone and strung with buffalo tendon. He also took a half-ounce lead ball from the pouch and wrapped the tendon around it as he stretched it tight.

The shot was ridiculously easy for Baylis, who could knock a hummingbird out of the air from 150 yards. Nor was there any question of a kill—a half-ounce ball could kill a buffalo. The rabbit suddenly shot straight up in the air, landed kicking, and then lay still. Later, when the sun was highest, he would spit it and roast it further back in the valley so his smoke couldn't be seen.

He was sure now that he knew where his enemy was. The other videttes might have spotted him, too. But he had one distinct advantage:

They all killed with firearms. Firearms meant plenty of noise, delays for reloading, and damp powder from dew and humidity.

He, in turn, had learned to kill silently and simply. He could hold ten balls in his left hand and fire them as fast as he could wrap them in the sling. He even knew how to shoot several balls at once for a volley effect.

So *let* them come. For something was coming their way, too: Death, on swift, silent wings of lightning.

Twenty feet beneath the bed of Salt Lick Creek, Seth Carlson's crew of sappers were literally changing the face of the West.

Carlson was damned proud of this idea. True, Hiram was the one financing it, as usual. But this time his military training had provided the perfect cover.

Carlson was a West Point graduate, as were a majority of the officers of that era. No matter what a West Point graduate eventually ended up doing for the Army, all of them received heavy doses of engineering training, both civil and combat. The War Department had first created its Corps of Engineers and Sappers in 1847 in response to the war with Mexico. Captain Robert E. Lee and others had engineered brilliant victories at Cerro Gordo and Chapultepec. Now all officers had some engineering behind them.

And Carlson had used that training to visualize a fortune.

Training his men as sappers—tunnel rats—

had been easy enough. So had the job of convincing Colonel Nearhood that a rainwater cistern must be built to help local farmers and sheepmen. Now his crews had a perfect cover for working in the field.

"Sir," said the trooper named Meadows, approaching Carlson where he stood inspecting the work. "We're runnin' scarce on shoring timbers."

"All right. Take a couple men and go cut some more. But *don't* haul them anywhere near the barn until after dark. Just pile them. If anybody should ask, you're cutting cooking wood for the work party at the cistern."

"Right, sir. Mum's the word."

Both men wore steel helmets with fat candles recessed into the front, miner's hats Hiram had provided. Although gun-cotton torches burned here and there, it was constantly dark in the tunnel. Dark and dank and still dangerous—the shoring was minimal, and the soil around it sometimes unstable.

The plan was simple and already starting to work. Using a tunnel the entire width of the creek as their staging area, they were able to plant underground explosives at key spots where the bed of Salt Lick Creek was already unstable. These were planted in smaller tunnels—called curtains—running off the main tunnel.

The effect of these charges was to change the grade of the bed. This, in turn, slued more and more water off into an old creek bed nearby. This old bed crossed Hiram's land claim. Filled with clear mountain runoff, it would be the best "mother ditch" in Wyoming, perfect for an extensive irrigation system.

But that new creek would do much more than make the two of them big nabobs around here. It would, by becoming the new and official Salt Lick Creek, eliminate a huge portion of the Northern Cheyenne homeland. And just as a rising tide lifts all the boats, a lowering creek would sink that goddamn Matthew Hanchon. Sink the red bastard once and for all.

Hot rage suffused his face as Carlson recalled all the times that damned savage had made a fool of him. The worst of it, of course, was Kristen Steele. That she could actually choose a filthy featherhead over an officer of the U.S. Army was galling enough.

But there was more. Fortunes lost because of Hanchon, promotions passed over, choice assignments given to other men after Hanchon marred his military record.

Oh, the list of offenses was long. Long indeed. And Seth Carlson brooked humiliation from no man.

Carlson relaxed somewhat as he thought about the scene topside, where Salt Lick Creek was starting to overflow its south bank. Soon, as Wolf Who Hunts Smiling liked to say, the worm would turn.

When the insects stop their chorus, then comes trouble.

The words were Arrow Keeper's, and suddenly they snapped in Touch the Sky's memory like burning twigs.

He dropped the paint's reins, halting her, and lifted one hand to stop Little Horse. Holding his finger to his lips to silence his curious friend, Touch the Sky made a careful examination of the area around them.

They had just entered the east side of Blackford's Valley, still tracking the river. The confluence with Salt Lick Creek was still out of sight ahead. Trees and grass and new wildflowers surrounded them here, the cover adequate if not excellent.

First Touch the Sky examined everything with a straight-on inspection. Then he turned sideways to study the same terrain from the corner of his eyes—sometimes that angle revealed things the other could not. He watched for motion, not shape. But nothing alerted him.

He knelt, touched the ground lightly with three fingertips. Nothing. No vibrations.

Finally he stood and smelled deeply of the air, for he had learned to detect the telltale odors of danger—especially white man's horses.

"Nothing," he told his friend finally. "Have I missed anything?"

Little Horse, who had been similarly searching around them, shook his head. "Perhaps an ant crawling on a log, brother, but nothing more."

"Still," Touch the Sky said, musing, "something is wrong."

But what? Jays chattered unconcerned nearby, a badger dug busily at the nearby bank, gray squirrels chased each other from cotton-wood to cottonwood. Nothing to suggest trouble.

The two friends chucked up their ponies and rode on. They eased through a dogleg bend in the river, and abruptly Touch the Sky noticed it: The insect hum had suddenly fallen silent, as abruptly as a door shutting.

He whirled around. Little Horse, sensing nothing, still moved forward toward him.

Touch the Sky felt the nape of his neck tingle, and now it *was* the shaman sense. He reacted without thinking.

Even as he started to roll off his pony's back, he tugged his red-streamered lance from its rigging. He swung the lance hard toward Little Horse, catching him across the chest and sweeping him off his mount. At the same time, as he crashed to the ground, Touch the Sky smacked his paint across the rump, sending him ahead into cover.

"Brother!" Little Horse protested. "What are you—"

There was no gunshot, just a hard, solid *thwack*. A big chunk of wood tore loose from a tree just behind the spot where Touch the Sky's head had been. Still sprawled on the ground, Little Horse turned pale even as more lethal projectiles made both braves roll for better cover.

Chapter Four

Hiram Steele was formidable even when he was in a good mood. But when he was angry, he was truly frightening. His face bloated like an image in a brass knob, his breath came in ragged gasps, and his voice came straight from his barrel chest.

And he was definitely angry now.

"Goddamnit straight to Hell and back!" he roared, his voice scaring some sparrows out of the far corners of the big barn. "It's happening all over again, Seth. In spite of everything, it's happening all over again."

Carlson frowned. He had been sweating like a dog down in the work shaft, and he was in no mood for Steele's tantrums. A streak of clay now matted Carlson's tow hair to one side of his head, and he was pale lately from lack of sleep and sunshine.

"Come down off your hind legs, Hiram," he snapped. "Baylis came here to tell you Hanchon has finally come. He's doing his job. Why kick dirt on his boots?"

"His job was to kill the red bastard, not announce his arrival like the Queen of England was here!"

Carlson sneered. "Hey? How many times have you botched it, Chief? How many times has the Wolf come a cropper trying to do for Hanchon? What about those ugly bastards Sis-ki-dee and Big Tree? You counted their coup feathers? Yet how many times have they aimed at Hanchon and hit only his shadow? And now you're all over Baylis like ugly on a buzzard, all on account that he missed his first shot?"

"Hell," Baylis added deferentially, "that's why we got so many men out there, ain't it, Mr. Steele? You yourself said this one slides through ambushes like grease through a goose."

"That's the straight, Mr. Steele," said Tim Ulrick. He was one of the sharpshooters serving as a sniper at the bluffs overlooking Salt Lick Creek and the valley. "Hell, ol' Baylis here was the first one to spot that tricky sumbitch. He's a good man to have along, even if he is a 'breed."

It was true that Hiram had an explosive temper. But like many volatile men, he could also see the error of his ways—especially when they threatened his profits.

"You boys are right," he conceded. "Baylis, I'd

ride the river with you any day. But all of us have got to see this thing right, see it for what it is. *Listen* to me, boys!"

The sudden urgency in Hiram's voice commanded everyone's instant attention. Seth, Baylis, Ulrick, and the rest of the videttes and snipers called to this meeting all watched Steele like hungry cats. Below, a sapper's voice could be heard as he hollered out for a light. The final charges would soon be in place. Tonight or the next night at the latest, they would detonate enough nitroglycerine to finish their task of changing the grade of the creek bed.

"All right, he got past Baylis. Now he's here. Here in the valley, and God knows there's enough places for him and that buck with him to cover down."

"Take my word for it," Carlson said. "I fought Hanchon down on the Staked Plain. He found cover where a lizard couldn't."

Steele nodded. "And he's not afraid to fight at night, like most Injins are. So I figure that's what he'll do. That limits our snipers, obviously. Even so, Tim, I want all four of you to remain up on the bluffs. Hanchon won't sleep *all* day. And a tangle or two with his good buddies Siski-dee and Big Tree will drive him back to daytime attacks. Baylis?"

"Yo?"

"You six videttes are critically important now. Stay in motion. Keep up fixed patterns that will keep Hanchon from surprising the barn. Remember, we can fail at this and we can fail at that. But if he breaches this spot before we can

44

cover the evidence inside, the fat will be in the fire for my Pikestown scheme. I'd like to keep all you men on the payroll, you know that. Pikestown will need good lawmen and whatnot."

"All that," Carlson said, "is true enough. But if Hanchon surprises us in that tunnel . . ."

He did not bother to finish the thought. If even a cornered mouse would fight, what might that savage do in a tunnel?

"I'm not moving from this place," Steele averred. "If he does find that tunnel, Seth boy, it'll be over my dead body."

Carlson said, "The main thing is, we won't need it much longer. Couple more days, then we can seal it off. We'll still need the barn to store tools and live in while we complete the aboveground operation after dark."

Again Hiram nodded, looking a little more optimistic again.

"Okay, boys, get back to it. Don't forget that huge stack of double eagles for the man who lets daylight into Hanchon's soul. We're a team here, and this time we're going to turn our fighting cock into a capon!"

Several times Little Horse had hinted how he would like to know more about the omen vision Touch the Sky had recently reported—the portent of trouble by water. But each time, Touch the Sky only shook his head and said quietly, "Leave it alone, brother."

Little Horse was strong, but Touch the Sky would never tell him or any living man what had been placed over his eyes. Yet he himself was doomed to relive the vision over and over.

It began innocently enough. He, Little Horse, Two Twists, and Tangle Hair had stopped to let their ponies drink from a wide, placid river of clear mountain runoff. The banks were lush, rolling grass, the water sweet and refreshing as they lay on the bank and dipped their heads into it.

Suddenly, Little Horse disappeared into the water, followed by Two Twists and Tangle Hair. Touch the Sky alone remained on the bank. Puzzled, he stood, waded in, looked for his friends, saying, "The joke is over, brothers!" And then his puzzlement quickly turned to a throat-clenching panic when none of them re-surfaced.

Each time, the vision was the same. Touch the Sky swallowed air, knifed into the cool current, kicked under. Searching, searching. There, a dark opening of some sort just ahead! When he swam toward it, a wall of bubbles engulfed him. He could see nothing.

Finally breaking clear, he glimpsed a beaded moccasin ahead—his comrades! Desperately Touch the Sky swam forward, reaching, grasping. His hand felt the elkskin moccasin, then an ankle. He tugged, a body rolled over, and abruptly a dead, grinning skull wearing Little Horse's clan feather bumped into Touch the Sky's face!

Each time that happened, Touch the Sky would mercifully start awake. He did so again now, and saw a worried Little Horse staring at him in the moonlight.

"The omen again, shaman?"

Touch the Sky nodded, sitting up. He had slept comfortably, if fitfully, on a dense carpet of pine needles hidden behind a deadfall.

"How is your arm?" he said, changing the subject.

"What, this mosquito bite? I would expect a woman to ask, but not you." When Touch the Sky swept him off his pony during the recent attack, Little Horse had landed on a sharp rock.

Touch the Sky grinned at this insult—Little Horse was in his usual fighting fettle. The tall Cheyenne pulled his Sharps percussion rifle from the buffalo robe protecting it from damp. He made sure a cap was positioned on the nib behind the hammer and the powder in his charger was dry.

"What now?" Little Horse asked. "We scout?"

Touch the Sky nodded. "We scout. So far, brother, we are not even sure *what* we are up against, though we know who must be behind it. We'll move back down to the creek. You take one bank, I the other. Give the owl hoot if you find anything."

Little Horse nodded, slinging his scattergun over one shoulder. Neither brave said a word about it, but Mother Night did not smile on her Indian children when they left the safety of the fire after darkness. And to die at night, away from camp, was to die unclean.

"Brother?" Little Horse said as they headed toward the little clearing where they'd tethered their ponies.

"I have ears, buck."

"If you are killed this night . . ."

47

He paused, and Touch the Sky watched him solemnly, expecting another question about his awful dream vision.

"May I smoke the fine white man's tobacco hidden in your parfleche?"

Touch the Sky felt a grin dividing his face. "Indeed. In fact, you may take it if I am only badly wounded and likely to die."

"In that case," Little Horse reasoned, "why not give it to me now, for you must die some day, am I right?"

Touch the Sky laughed outright as he handed it over. "The white man's lawyers could not talk around you! Now give over with all this talk, stout brave, and come earn your tobacco."

The main thing was to find out exactly who they were up against, and then exactly *what* they were up against. So far Touch the Sky had nothing he could place in his parfleche.

The *who* could be surmised, although as that silent slingshot attack proved, there were always new people on Hiram Steele's side. But so far Touch the Sky had no inkling as to the *what*. There was no link between the mystery of the river's shallow level and the presence of his enemies—no link he had discovered, at any rate.

But old Arrow Keeper had spoken straight when he'd said, "The hand that whirls the water in the pool also stirs the quicksand." Proof or no, Touch the Sky's gut hunch and his shaman sense told him the river and Steele were indeed linked. And why attack here, at the edge of Blackford's Valley, unless there was something to hide? There were better spots for killing him. Why here?

"Brother," he had said to Little Horse while they made their preparations for a night scout. "This valley is big. A man might need nine or ten sleeps to explore it well. Where would you start?"

"When we are involved," Little Horse said bluntly, "always start where trouble is the thickest and danger at its worst. Start by staying near the river. I believe your omen. This is trouble by water. When are we shy to meet trouble?"

"Indeed, it comes to us if we don't visit regularly. But you are right, buck. The river. And no better place to start than the confluence where Salt Lick Creek joins the Powder."

So they bore that way now, though keeping well back from the river. They had already seen telltale signs that the river was being patrolled. What bothered Touch the Sky was the fact that they did not see *many* signs. This enemy was good. He recalled an old saying about the Southwest Apaches: "Worry when you see them. Worry even more when you don't."

They had anticipated night fighting when they chose their ponies, avoiding any light markings that would reflect moonlight. The two braves now prepared themselves by wrapping their eyes in blankets—when they finally unwrapped them, their night vision had improved dramatically. They smeared their arms, chests, and faces with dark river clay to cut reflection.

A cloud-obstructed three-quarter moon provided some light, though the canopy of trees overhead often interrupted it. Slowly, stopping often to look and listen and smell, the two braves advanced toward the confluence.

Touch the Sky and Little Horse had connected their wrists with a light sisal rope. Suddenly Touch the Sky felt a sharp tug as Little Horse warned him to halt. He dropped the paint's reins, and she stopped immediately.

Now Touch the Sky noticed what had alerted Little Horse: the faint chinking of bit rings. Riders—white men, probably—down near the river.

More patrollers, Touch the Sky thought grimly. Not necessarily looking for him, but certainly looking for somebody. Or perhaps more accurately, making sure no one discovered something they weren't supposed to discover.

The two warriors remained still, weapons to hand, until the riders had passed by, riding south.

"Glide like a shadow now," Touch the Sky whispered close in his friend's ear. "We are near."

The tall Cheyenne felt his heart hammering; felt, too, the sure knowledge that danger lived in this valley—terrible danger, more than the silence and solitude could prepare one to believe. They had faced death here once before. This time, however, death was back with fresh legions.

The two warriors hobbled their ponies foreleg to rear. Then, moving like stalking cats, they covered the rest of the distance to the confluence on foot. They had to negotiate rough thick-

ets, tangled briars, deadfalls, and boggy
backwaters.

They stepped into a small, moonlit clearing.
Little Horse pointed ahead. The shadowy mass
of an old hay barn, sagging like a swayback
mule, loomed off to the right, perhaps a double
stone's throw back from the confluence of Salt
Lick Creek and the Powder.

Touch the Sky paid little attention to the
barn. They had searched it during their last vigil
in this valley. It had obviously been abandoned
for years, and was pitch black and silent now.
He was more concerned with studying the sooty
darkness surrounding the confluence. They
would have to move in close for any kind of useful examination.

Yet, the nape of his neck throbbed warmly—a
familiar sign to Touch the Sky, and one he had
learned to heed.

"Brother," he whispered, "call on your medicine now. We're moving closer. But all is not as
lonely and quiet as it appears."

Little Horse did touch the medicine pouch on
his sash and say a brief, silent prayer. But he
also double-checked the mizzen and pan of all
four barrels of his scattergun, rotating them to
check the action. No sound was worse to a warrior than the fizzle of damp powder at the ulti-
mate moment.

The two moved out, side by side, holding
their sisal rope snug for instant, silent com-
munication.

The water brawled noisily, for even low as it
was now, the Powder was a good-sized river

and Salt Lick Creek had considerable flow this early in the warm moons. They could hear the combined sound out ahead of them, a steady bubbling and sighing.

Abruptly, another noise joined the water sound, subtle at first. So subtle that Touch the Sky strained to verify it in the darkness.

But it was real.

Laughter. Deliberate, mocking laughter. Close by, yet seeming to come from everywhere at once, the airy mocking of ghosts.

Little Horse, too, heard it. And like Touch the Sky, he recovered in an eyeblink and knew full well it was no ghost. They both knew who it was, and it was no discredit to their manhood when a ball of solid ice replaced their stomachs.

"Laughing again, Sis-ki-dee?" Touch the Sky spoke out boldly, knowing it was no use to hold silence now. "I am glad you have become sassy again. You may recall, the last time I saw you, up in Bloody Bones Canyon, you were not laughing. Your face was screwed up like a bawling baby's as you begged me to spare your life. Since, unlike you, I do not kill puling infants, I was forced to let you go."

With a faint whisper of warning, Touch the Sky threw his head back. Something burned his chin, and then he heard a sudden crack as Sis-ki-dee's war lance chunked into a tree beside him.

"Most of what you said just now was lies, Noble Red Man!" came Sis-ki-dee's voice boldly out of the darkness. "Except the part about killing puling babies. You see, that is why I am

52

laughing as I watch you and Horse's Ass crawl through the mud like Big Indians on the warpath. I could have killed both of you long ago. But that would ruin my great joy. For you see, Noble Red Man, you have been lured from your camp so that Big Tree could gut your woman and child!"

Chapter Five

A twig snapped somewhere in the deep darkness surrounding the tipi, and Honey Eater started awake.

She could feel her heart pulsing in her throat. She glanced beside her on the spread-out robes, and saw that Little Bear slept soundly on his belly.

She felt her face tug into a grin, despite her fear, at the sight of the white columbine petal stuck to his chin. Tiny tooth marks on it told her he had tried to eat it.

On the other side of the tipi's center pole, she could hear her aunt, Sharp Nosed Woman, snoring softly. She always stayed with her aunt when Touch the Sky rode out from camp. All seemed well. Especially when she realized that the snapping twig must have been either Tangle

Hair or Two Twists—she could hear both of them outside now, whispering quietly. She knew they were taking turns guarding the tipi.

That knowledge calmed her at first, despite the deep fear she felt for her husband. No one would touch her or her son while those two were on guard.

But though they spoke low, she could not help hearing what they said. And listening to them, Honey Eater tasted the copper bile of fear.

"Did you notice who rode back earlier?" the voice of Two Twists asked.

"I did, double-braid," Tangle Hair answered. "Our tribe's best self-proclaimed 'policeman.' Did you see him cut out two fresh ponies from his string?"

"I did. Wolf Who Hunts Smiling has taken nothing but war mounts. He means to send our comrades under or please the Wendigo trying."

"They are up against it," Tangle Hair agreed. "But never mind the temptation to join them. As much as they must need us, this camp is teetering on the brink of its own grave. If Touch the Sky is killed, the Bull Whips will move instantly here. You know that, don't you?"

"As surely as I know my clan notch," Two Twists said reluctantly. "With those renegades sitting on top of Wendigo Mountain, we are mice with only one hole. They, too, are up to some treachery. There have been smoke and mirror signals between them and Wolf Who Hunts Smiling."

A long silence followed while Honey Eater

felt the nauseous flutter of despair.

"Still," Tangle Hair added, and his words made her face go clammy with sweat, "Touch the Sky's omen of a hard death by water is yet cankering at me."

At Sis-ki-dee's goading words about Honey Eater and Little Bear, Touch the Sky felt a quick spike of panic.

"Steady, shaman," Little Horse whispered beside him even as they ducked for quick cover. "This is their old game. Let them unstring your nerves now, and we are gone beavers. Answer them, buck!"

Touch the Sky knew his stout friend was right again. Sis-ki-dee excelled at finding the single chink in a man's armor, and then pounding away at it.

"Always harping on my woman and child," Touch the Sky called out. Like his friend's, his own eyes desperately searched the thickly wooded and overgrown area surrounding them. But even with their night vision improved, they could see no one. "When you aren't boasting of topping a man's wife, you boast of killing her. No tribe, not even the filthy Diggers, is lower than you 'contrary warriors.' "

"As for your mighty woman-killer named Big Tree," Little Horse put in, leveling his scatter-gun at the darkness, "unless he has eaten peyote, he certainly knows better than to enter a Cheyenne camp. Our dogs know the Comanche stink. Big Tree is cowering there with you, Red Peril."

"I am here, Horse's Ass," Big Tree's voice boomed out. "But not cowering. And I will top your mother while you watch."

"And you, Wolf Who Hunts Smiling," Touch the Sky shouted. "Are you enjoying this sport, licker of white feet?"

An arrow whipped by Touch the Sky, passing only inches away from his head.

"It is more interesting than picking lice from my blanket," Wolf Who Hunts Smiling answered boldly. "But as for sport, that has not even begun, Noble Red Man. I play the dog for no white man. I bend them to my purpose. After they help me kill you, I will kill them."

"Yes," Touch the Sky scoffed, trying to purchase time in hopes of spotting their enemies. "Your famous war of extermination. You green-antlered fool! I heard your lackey Medicine Flute swear to the people that the white man's land east of the Great Waters is smaller than a buffalo range! You fools preach they are a small tribe and can be eliminated in one good battle. In truth, there are ten thousand hair-faces for every Indian. You would have better luck stamping out a prairie fire in a windstorm than eliminating the beef-eaters."

A rifle spoke its piece—Sis-ki-dee's North & Savage, Touch the Sky judged from the sharp, precise crack. The slug was several feet off target, and he breathed a little easier. Sis-ki-dee was a good marksmen and wouldn't shoot that wide unless he was guessing at his target.

"The noble savage lectures us!" Big Tree called out sarcastically. "He knows so much

57

about the paleface world because he, too, once worked in the garden like a woman and wore shoes and gorged on beef and pig meat. Now he ruts on an Indian beauty and calls himself a shaman."

Touch the Sky tugged the sisal rope to alert Little Horse. When his friend glanced at him, Touch the Sky rolled his head over his left shoulder, toward the horses behind them. Little Horse nodded, agreeing this was a time to withdraw, not to dig in for their own slaughter.

"I know much indeed about the paleface world," Touch the Sky said. "I know about engineering charges, for instance."

Not one of his enemies said anything to this remark, and Touch the Sky didn't welcome that silence. It confirmed his suspicion that they were teamed up with Steele and probably Carlson. He and Little Horse had not yet gotten close enough to the confluence for a better look, and clearly they would not do so this night.

His enemies chose this moment to open up in earnest. Big Tree and Wolf Who Hunts Smiling unleashed a flurry of arrows, and Sis-ki-dee's North & Savage roared again and again, its sliding magazine letting him fire every few seconds.

"*Now*, brother!" Touch the Sky roared, and Little Horse sent up a virtual wall of buckshot as he fired and rotated, fired and rotated, peppering the trees with four deadly charges.

This formidable firepower sent their enemies scrambling just long enough for the two braves to break from their meager cover and race toward their ponies. But Touch the Sky hardly felt elated by it.

They were safe for the moment, yes. But they knew nothing about the mystery of the disappearing river. All they knew for sure was that every step taken in this valley of death was another step closer to the funeral scaffold.

"We may have hit one of them," Big Tree suggested.

"Are *you* eager to go search the underbrush for proof?" Sis-ki-dee demanded.

"If one was hit, either he was killed or he wasn't," Wolf Who Hunts Smiling said. "If he was killed, his comrade would not leave the body for us to desecrate, count upon it. If he was not killed, then he would never have been deserted by his comrade. These are 'noble' red brothers who cry when a child dies. In short, bucks, either no one is out there or we killed both of them."

All three saw the absurdity of this latter suggestion. Those two Cheyennes would not be killed in a game of shooting-at-rovers. The killing would be hard and the dying important.

The trio was well hidden behind blinds constructed earlier in anticipation of this moment. Behind them, silver-white moonlight gleamed off the swirling waters at the confluence of Salt Lick Creek and the Powder river.

"They have not shown a light from the barn," Big Tree said. "Steele spoke one way when he swore he would not give their presence away. He has staked his sash to the ground, for he means this time to kill the tall one."

"Steele is a Mah-ish-ta-shee-da," Wolf Who Hunts Smiling said, using the ancient Cheyenne name for white men. "And of course he will die with the rest. But he is a good man to have along on any mission to kill Touch the Sky."

Sis-ki-dee's brass nose ring caught a stray shaft of moonlight. "What will they do next?" he asked.

Automatically, the other two waited for Wolf Who Hunts Smiling to answer. After all, he knew their enemy best—had in fact hated him the longest and with the most reason.

"They will complete tonight's mission, which was to examine that confluence. It hardly matters if they do study it—all they will see is Mother Earth getting a slight wrinkle in her skin. They will see that Salt Lick Creek is altering its course into the old tributary it used to follow. It will seem the work of the High Holy Ones, and no Indian will question it."

"We could track them at first light and find their camp," Sis-ki-dee said.

"Have you been skull-struck?" Wolf Who Hunts Smiling demanded. "Would you trail a grizzly into its lair? Besides, they will change their camps often. We are all three excellent at reading sign. But this is no time for stalking. It is a time for luring."

The other two watched him in the imperfect moonlight, unable to decipher his lupine grin. Even now Wolf Who Hunts Smiling's swift-asminnow eyes stayed in constant motion, watching for attack.

"Luring?" Big Tree repeated. "Are you a little girl dropping coy hints in her sewing lodge? Speak it or bury it, Cheyenne. I am in no mood for riddles."

"No riddle, Quohada. Only think. Steele is determined to keep these new intruders away from the huge lodge where his people are sheltered. Naturally they fear any discovery while they are down in their tunnel. But what if I can convince Steele *not* to fill in the tunnel when they finish with it, which they will do within a few sleeps."

Sis-ki-dee's crazy laughter showed that he had caught on—and that he approved. "Leave the tunnel, you mean, and lure Touch the Sky and Little Horse into it?"

Wolf Who Hunts Smiling nodded, grinning. "Lure them into their underwater graves. One charge, exploded after they go in, would both close the tunnel and bring the water rushing in."

A long silence followed this as all three Indians savored the prospect.

"This would be more than revenge," Big Tree finally said. "Knowing that we had trapped Touch the Sky's soul in torment for eternity. Not just revenge—this is a reason to have lived!"

"Never mind gloating now," Wolf Who Hunts Smiling warned them. "Our work this night may not be done. The hair-faces are detonating another underground charge, their last of the underground labor. It may bring our enemies back around."

"Perhaps," Big Tree said. "But I think not. Now that Touch the Sky knows he faces us by night, he may decide that he would rather face videttes and snipers by day. He and Little Horse will return to the confluence, yes. But it will be boldly, in broad daylight."

"They threw everything they had at us," Little Horse boasted, trying to put a good face on their inglorious retreat. "And we made off unscathed. No scalps dangle from our sashes, but at least ours are still in place on our heads."

"As you say, brother," Touch the Sky agreed. "And we have cheated them again as we did on Wendigo Mountain. Too, our mission tonight was no complete waste—at least we learned there must be something worth seeing near that confluence."

The two weary braves had just finished rubbing their ponies down with clumps of sage. Now the horses were tethered in a hidden spot well back from the river, logy with long drinks of cool river water. The Cheyennes themselves had sheltered in a crude wickiup that resembled, from a distance, a tangled deadfall.

Now they eased the gnawing in their bellies with dried fruit and slices of pemmican.

"I will risk a night mission," Touch the Sky said, "if the good of it outweighs the risk of it. But the worst time in the world to face Big Tree or Sis-ki-dee is after sunset. As for Wolf Who Hunts Smiling, *he* is in killing fettle night or day. I counsel for sleeping the rest of this night and riding out by daylight."

Little Horse agreed. "We will make easier targets, but we will also draw easier beads on our enemies. I would rather shoot at a man than at his voice."

Both braves slipped into their own thoughts while the river chuckled and bubbled nearby—the river, source of all life but now the source of much danger. Once or twice, as they lay quiet, Touch the Sky heard a vidette rider down near the water.

But eventually his tense muscles relaxed enough to permit a fitful sleep. Thankfully, Mai-yun did not plague him again this night with images of that death-by-water omen.

Uncle Moon owned the sky and was clawing his way toward his zenith, when the earth literally heaved the Indians awake.

It was not a loud, violent explosion. Instead the ground suddenly shifted hard, like a canoe running aground on a sandbar. A brief rumble, like the sound of a distant avalanche, and it was over. Both Cheyennes started to a sitting position, staring at each other in the moonlight.

"Brother?" Little Horse called over. "What happened?"

"How long is a piece of string?" Touch the Sky answered glumly. "But whatever it was, Cheyenne, count upon it: It means a world of hurt for the red man."

Chapter Six

"There it is, Seth boy," Hiram Steele said jubilantly, thumping the grinning soldier hard between the shoulder blades. "There it goddamn is! The gateway to Pikestown and our fortune!"

"Last night's blast did it," Carlson confirmed. "Look at it! I should have been an engineer, not a combat officer! Not one sign that man has been tinkering. All the changes are below, in the slant and thickness of the bed."

Even Wolf Who Hunts Smiling was truly impressed. You could say many things against white men. They always screamed at each other, even when standing close; they showed their emotions in their faces like women; they wore shoes and wasted buffalo meat and built their fires all wrong. But while an Indian was forced to circle around a mountain, the hair-faces simply blew the mountain out of their way, as *this* impressive sight proved.

Dawn threw her first roseate glow over the new day, light enough to see that the former bed of Salt Lick Creek was now virtually dry save for some isolated pools dotting the drying mud. The creek had evidently jumped its old bank and now followed the course of the old tributary that bore due south from here.

"Goddamn dirty shame, ain't it?" Hiram said with mock sympathy. "I mean, my land suddenly water rich, and them poor Northern Cheyennes about to lose most of their summer water."

If he hoped to prick Wolf Who Hunts Smiling with this barb, he failed. Let River of Wind's camp dry up, the renegade's approving eyes proclaimed. He would soon be joining the Comanche and Blackfeet raiders on Wendigo Mountain. Once he did, Hiram Steele and his white brothers would be killed or driven from this territory anyway.

"This is impressive work," the Cheyenne conceded to the palefaces. "We Indians have no medicine like it. But if you wish to remain in the land of the living, I advise both of you to get out of the open. Do you think the tall one is not watching both of you right now through a rifle sight?"

Steele and Carlson were not men to scare easily. But the sense of Wolf Who Hunts Smiling's words struck each of them with the force of a blow. They took cover like the Cheyenne.

"Where's Big Tree and Sis-ki-dee?" Steele demanded.

"Do I look like their dug nurse?" Wolf Who Hunts Smiling retorted. "Presumably they are sleeping—you kept them up all night. What does it matter where they are? Do not count on other men to save your own hair. Touch the Sky has tried more than once to kill me, but each time *I* was ready."

"Yeah, yeah, you're a big Indian," Carlson said with contempt. "Lecturing white men now, is it? He hasn't sent me or Hiram under yet either. I don't need no goddamn lectures from an aboriginal gut-eater too stupid to harness the wheel."

"Both of you come down off your hind legs," Hiram said, though he was still in a good mood. "Our first priority is to kill Hanchon, remember? Once we put paid to him, then we can scrap all we want 'mongst ourselves."

Hiram turned to the officer. "I'll be going into Register Cliffs to sign on some more homesteaders. Do we need the tunnel anymore?"

Seth shook his head. Much of his face was in shadow under the wide brim of his hat.

"All right, then," Hiram said, "have your boys fill it back up."

"That," said Wolf Who Hunts Smiling, "would be foolish."

Both white men were surprised that the Indian had spoken up about this.

"Another damn lecture," Carlson said.

"Unless you got a bone caught in your throat," Steele said, "speak your piece."

"It is foolish to waste the tunnel," Wolf Who Hunts Smiling said. "Of course it must be filled in. But why not fill it up after Touch the Sky and Little Horse find it and go down to explore it?"

Seth looked at Hiram. Hiram suddenly grinned. Seth grinned back.

"Well, now," Carlson said. "You both know goddamn good and well they *will* go into it if they find it. If we let them find it."

"Wolf," Hiram said admiringly, "I'm beginning to realize what a waste it will be if I kill you. You're right, buck. No sense wasting a good grave that's got Hanchon's name on it."

"There they are," Little Horse said bitterly. "Three of our worst enemies in the world. Not one of them exposed to a good shot. If the Wendigo puked up Big Tree and Sis-ki-dee, they would all be congregated in one place. And tomorrow, count upon it, the grass where they stood would be dead."

Touch the Sky nodded. Both braves clung to a dead log out in the middle of the Powder River. They had slipped into the water shortly after sunrise, using reeds to breathe and staying submerged as they drifted along.

Now only their heads protruded out of the streaming current. Their enemy had posted sentries and roaming skirmishers everywhere. But the one place they did not watch well was the river itself.

"Of the three you are looking at now," Touch the Sky said, "it is Wolf Who Hunts Smiling

67

who has set the mark for treachery. True, those two white-eyed pigs are criminals of the lowest kind. But even they are loyal to their own. Yet our wily Wolf has sullied the Medicine Arrows beyond cleansing by shedding blood of his own. And now, only look. Another kind of lifeblood is being bled from our people—our very river."

At least they had finally solved part of the mystery of the receding river level. Salt Lick Creek had evidently leaped its bank, costing the Powder its major feeder between the foothills and the Cheyenne summer camp. The Powder still had plenty of flow right here, but would lose much of this water downriver.

"We may face a drought by the time of the hot moons," Little Horse said. "The entire camp will have to be moved."

Touch the Sky said nothing to this, only watching that unholy trio gloating over their latest triumph. But was it truly their work? What, exactly, did they have to do with it? There was no outward sign of damming or digging.

Little Horse's thoughts, too, wandered in the same direction. "That explosion we heard— why is there no damage here? No dirt heaved out of place?"

"Brother, you ask all the right questions. But I have none of the right answers."

"We signed the talking papers at Fort Laramie," Little Horse said, referring to the latest peace treaty. "That paper forbids the hair-faces from any tampering with the rivers and creeks that cross our land. But first we must have proof they are playing the foxes."

"The talking papers," Touch the Sky repeated, and suddenly heat rushed into his face as he understood the real depth of this new threat.

Little Horse saw the troubled clouds in his friend's dark eyes. "What, brother? What did I say?"

"That same talking paper," Touch the Sky replied grimly, "sets out the boundary of our ranges. It is bounded on the east by 'the deepest point in the channel of Salt Lick Creek.' Do you understand now?"

It took Little Horse only a few heartbeats to comprehend. His face, too, went a few shades paler.

"Yes, I see it, brother. Clear as a blood spoor in new snow I see it. If they succeed in this treachery, we are not just out of water. We will lose over half of our land!"

Touch the Sky nodded. "The half where we hunt the best buffalo herds. The half containing the best graze for our pony herds. The half where we camp, where our women grow their best crops. The half where we gather each spring with the other nine bands of the Cheyenne for the parades and dances."

"The best half of our homeland," Little Horse summed up.

"And would it be a surprise if you learn," Touch the Sky said, "that the land now belongs to Hiram Steele? Belongs, at least, in the eyes of the white man's council."

Now both braves stared at the trio with a new sense of urgency.

"This is the worst trouble in the world," Little

Horse lamented. "We have little enough power in the white man's courts. Even when treaty violations are clear and easily proved, justice can be elusive. How will we defeat whites with no proof of their crime?"

"We won't," Touch the Sky said. "When it comes to justice, all we have is ourselves. We need to discover how they have done this, yes. But only so we can undo it. If we depend on the white-eyes' courts, we will end up on a reservation growing corn and answering roll calls."

"Undo it?" Little Horse repeated doubtfully.

"You heard me, stout buck. Undo it. Either we get Salt Lick Creek back to its old course, or we are a tribe without a home."

The morning passed uneventfully for Tim Ulrick.

He was one of the four sharpshooters Hiram Steele had hired to man the bluffs overlooking the river. It was lonely, boring work, but he didn't mind it. He had a dog tent and a waterproof Mackinaw blanket to protect him if it rained. He had plenty of beans and jerked beef and coffee and whiskey, as well as a stack of sensational dime novels to while away the hours. It beat the living hell out of his last job: riding guard for the Kansas-Pacific Railroad's work crews. Hell, he'd rather be the sniper than the target any damned day.

His rifle, a Hawken .54 buffalo gun, was set up on a bipod overlooking the river and much of Blackford's Valley. From here, when the sun was shining, he could send mirror flashes to the other three snipers.

The morning had been a slow one. Nothing on the river except an old dead log earlier. Just past forenoon the vidette named Baylis Morningstar rode by and shared a smoke with him. He, too, reported no sign of the Cheyennes.

Damn, Ulrick thought. That little breed was death-to-the-devil with that slingshot of his.

Ulrick could see clearly, from this high vantage point, how Salt Lick Creek now followed a new course. He didn't give a plugged peso for the fact that Indians would be displaced by this new project of Steele's, but it was a damn shame to see good rangeland plowed up for a bunch of damned fodder-forkers. And that was exactly what Steele had in mind: turning cattle country into cornfields and sheep pens.

Ulrick's thoughts suddenly dispersed like chaff in the wind as he noticed something below: another damned log, only further downriver this time. But just for a second there, he could have sworn he saw a glimpse of a human head.

He broke out his binoculars and focused them. There was the log, bobbing and weaving. Nothing out of the ordinary—

Wait. What the hell was that?

Ulrick focused even more and squinted.

He saw what looked like a thin reed poking up out of the water—following along on one side of the log.

An ear-to-ear grin split his beard-stubbled face. Ulrick had a sudden vision of that giant

71

stack of gold cartwheels Hiram was paying to the man who did for Matthew Hanchon.

Ulrick scrambled close to his Hawken and took up a prone position behind the weapon. He removed a paper cartridge from his possibles bag and chewed one end off it. He dumped the powder in his charger, inserted the ball and rammed it home, then placed a primer cap on the nib behind the hammer.

Ulrick licked one finger to test the wind. Then he made minor adjustments to his elevation and windage knobs.

Finally ready, he dug a hole with his left elbow until it was comfortable in the dirt. Then, training his sights just below that reed, he inserted his finger behind the trigger guard.

He took a deep breath, relaxed as he let it out. Slowly, squeezing and not jerking, he took up his trigger slack.

Touch the Sky and Little Horse knew they could not return overland to their cold camp in broad daylight. Nor could they float their log against the current without arousing suspicion. So they decided to float well past the confluence and then double back through the trees behind the most heavily patrolled area.

Touch the Sky held on at the back of the big log, Little Horse at the front. Both braves were built very differently, and Touch the Sky had the easier time staying submerged. From time to time he was forced to tap his friend to warn him that he was letting too much of himself show above water.

Out in the channel the river was deep enough to make the going fairly easy. From time to time they encountered a sawyer or other snags, and occasionally fish nibbled at them—an oddly distasteful sensation, considering its harmlessness and the fact that these two braves had faced every demon in the red man's world.

But both realized why it was distasteful. Cheyenne lore included a legend about Indians who died unclean deaths in the water. Their trapped souls were forced to watch while hungry fish nibbled out their dead eyes.

However, Touch the Sky admonished himself to forget such thoughts. The key to survival lay in attending to the present, not in dwelling on thoughts. His wife and son were only one sleep's distance further downriver, their fate too hinging on his success here in the valley.

Again he kicked forward with his right foot, tapping Little Horse. He was letting too much of his reed protrude.

Even as he warned his friend, Touch the Sky felt a sharp prick at his chest—sharper than the curious teeth of fish.

He glanced down and watched a swirl of blood rise up with the bubbles his feet kicked up!

His bear-claw necklace—the one Honey Eater gave him for a wedding gift! One of the claws was gouging into his flesh and muscle!

This was no time to evaluate the sign. Touch the Sky let go of the log, kicked mightily forward, gripped Little Horse around both hips, and tugged his surprised friend down.

73

There was a sharp concussive sound, magnified by the water, as the slug slanted in between both braves, missing each by a finger's breadth. And then both were kicking madly for the far bank, hoping there was only one shooter and praying to Maiyun he now had to reload.

Praying, too, that if they must die, Maiyun would let it be on land.

Chapter Seven

Clearly, Little Bear had gotten over his fear of the water, thought Honey Eater.

She watched her little son splashing and kicking, bravely plunging his head under the water to come up gasping. She shared for a moment in his harmless pleasure, happy for him. Like her, he missed his father. Moments like this helped take both their minds off his absence.

But not for long, Honey Eater thought glumly. A brief glance to either bank would show her the ever-faithful Tangle Hair and Two Twists. They would be at a discreet distance, yet close enough to intervene if there was trouble.

And the river itself . . . She and Little Bear had come down here to cool off, for the day was unseasonably hot by midday. But she had stared in shock. Its depth, already receding, had gone down dramatically, all in one night!

How could such things be, unless the hand of magic was in it? Or the white men with their powerful explosives? And that, of course, meant that Touch the Sky was up against it yet again.

Medicine Flute, the skinny little pretender, was making all kinds of trouble in camp. For Touch the Sky was gone, the river was drying up before their eyes, and the connection seemed obvious enough to her husband's many enemies—Touch the Sky must be causing this trouble.

Fortunately, Chief River of Winds was able to make cooler heads prevail. At the council meeting, he reminded the bickering headmen that Wolf Who Hunts Smiling, too, was out without permission of council. And if a Bull Whip soldier could ride out, he argued, how could one deny this privilege to the tribe's shaman?

But Honey Eater realized how quickly things could change in this unstable camp. Especially if the Powder continued to fall without explanation.

By now the people were terribly concerned. By night the old grandmothers had taken to keening into the early hours, sensing the arrival of some great tragedy. By day they had begun to sew together animal skins for storing water against a coming drought.

But Little Bear sensed none of this. Again his head broke the surface, sleek and shiny, his dark locks plastered to his forehead.

There! Honey Eater saw it clearly in this light when his hair was swept back, the mulberry colored birthmark on his left temple. Just like Touch the Sky, he had the mark of the arrow. He might enjoy his innocence now, she thought. But for him, too, a lifetime of fighting and killing was coming.

Fighting and killing. The very things Touch the Sky was no doubt enmeshed in right now. And Little Horse with him. If any two braves could make it back to camp, they were those two.

But how long? How long could they keep defeating the odds? She watched her healthy, innocent son splashing in the river. Then she glanced again at the clear marks on the banks which told the sad story of a river's disappearance.

Touch the Sky and Little Horse both made it to shore without stopping a slug from the hidden sniper up on the bluff.

"There was only one up there, brother," Touch the Sky said. "That saved us. Few men can recharge a rifle in less than thirty seconds. Good thing he did not have a second piece charged and to hand, for he is a formidable shot."

Little Horse nodded glumly. The two braves had made their way cautiously overland on foot, a distasteful way to travel for Plains warriors. The ground cover was good close to the river, but by now they realized they were surrounded by enemies with eyes like eagles.

So the journey was made cautiously, employing every trick of their warrior training in movement and concealment. In sparsely covered areas, they moved slowly, not quickly, for it was movement and not shape that caught an enemy's eye at a distance.

They were bearing obliquely toward the spot, near the entrance of Blackford's Valley, where they had hidden their ponies.

"Brother," Little Horse said, "when have you seen me sit upon the ground and wail? But this thing would be examined. We are marked for carrion in this valley! If we are unable to move, how can we name their game?"

Even as he spoke, he watched a nearby river bluff carefully. The two braves were easing through a blackberry thicket. It was good cover, but hard to move through.

Touch the Sky nodded. "It comes down to a hard truth, buck. By day we are targets for any who would kill us. By night we face Sis-ki-dee and Big Tree. And no doubt Wolf Who Hunts Smiling."

"The palefaces have the daylight covered," Little Horse said bitterly, "and their cowardly Indian dogs the night. Meantime, our river is drying up! And we may soon even be forced to desert our homeland if Steele goes to the white man's council with his new claim."

"Cheyenne," Touch the Sky admired, "you have cracked the shell and extracted the nut. We know more than we did. Now we must find out how that creek was forced out of its natural course. Once we know that, only then can we try to return things to normal."

"Brother," Little Horse reminded him. "We

have failed to approach that confluence by land. We have just been shot at trying by water. What next? Fly?"

Little Horse had spoken facetiously, but his words evoked a sly grin from Touch the Sky.

"Yes, stout buck. We will fly."

Clearly Little Horse wanted to hear more on this foolish theme. But Touch the Sky nodded toward the bluff again, reminding him it was time to tend to the language of the senses.

Sister Sun was well through the day's journey by the time they had caught up with their ponies and moved them to a new spot. Now it was time to return to their cold camp and retrieve their kits, then move to a new camp. Touch the Sky could feel hunger gnawing at his belly like a rat's incisors.

They showed extra caution as they approached the little copse where they had slept. They were approaching the entrance, a narrow opening in the brush, when Touch the Sky felt it: that graining of his skin that was not caused by fear or cold.

"Hold," he whispered to Little Horse. Both braves dropped to their knees, examining the area around them carefully.

Little Horse gripped his friend's shoulder and pointed. Touch the Sky sighted along his companion's finger and saw a tangled vine just out ahead of them. It appeared, at first glance, to belong to the natural confusion of brush carpeting the ground.

"It is too green and fresh," Little Horse whispered. "It was broken off and placed there for some reason. The rest of the vines are all old and dead, see?"

Touch the Sky nodded. He reached to one side and pulled a long stick up from the dead brush. Then he moved forward and gave it a thrust toward the vine.

It tripped the hidden deadfall trap immediately. A bent sapling, hidden behind bigger trees, suddenly whipped straight, taking its empty net of vines with it.

Touch the Sky recognized Cheyenne handiwork here. And he knew the trap had not been erected simply to annoy them. The moment the vine net cleared the treetops, an arrow whipped through it. Moments later came the drum of escaping hooves.

Little Horse retrieved the shaft.

"Look," he said, pointing to the chipped flint point. "Made by our tribe. Are you surprised?"

"Wolf Who Hunts Smiling," Touch the Sky said grimly, his lips pressed into a straight, determined slit. "He had it all set up, then found a good spot to wait."

It made both of them nervous that he had been able to track down this camp. After all, it had been used only one night. Would they now have to change camps every few hours?

Touch the Sky glanced around at the surrounding valley walls in the waning light. This was a place of great natural beauty. But for them it had become a death trap. Those walls seemed to be pressing in on them, and it was only a matter of time before they would be caught, then crushed.

"Never mind," he said. "The fight goes forward. We will move to a new spot. Then, after the sun goes to her rest, we will return to that confluence."

"Yes," Little Horse said skeptically. "And we will be 'flying' there as you promised, right?"

"Like two jays."

"Shaman tricks?" Little Horse pressed.

"Only Medicine Flute will tell you he can truly fly," Touch the Sky said. "No shaman tricks this time. You will see. Now move quickly, brother, and keep both eyes to the sides."

"Gentlemen," Hiram Steele told the men gathered around him at the bar, "the sun travels west, and so does opportunity. This new Homestead Act gives all of you a nice parcel of ground, and all you have to do is prove it up a little and it's yours."

"Nice parcel, my sweet aunt," groused a man with a heavy Swedish accent. "A hunnert and forty-four acres is a big farm back East, ya sure. But this ground out here, why, she's dry as a year-old cow chip! You can't farm it. She's only good for ranching, and you can't ranch on less than ten times that much land."

"Correction, my friend," Hiram said, pouring the man out another shot of good grain mash. "The ground *was* dry as a year-old cow chip. Not anymore. It will soon be well irrigated."

"Ahuh," said another man. "And the Queen of England will sing 'Lulu Girl' at the mining camp on Bear Creek!"

"Friend, I speak straight-arrow. You've heard

that Salt Lick Creek has jumped its bank? That it follows an old bed south from its old route?"

"Ya sure," said the Swede. "Goddamnedest thing it was, too. But fella, that's not government ground it goes through. That's Injin land."

"It was," Hiram assured him. "But the boundary was determined by the old course of the creek. Fact is, that new feeder goes right across *my* grantland. And now the plots around it are up for grabs. All you need to do is get your butts into Register Cliffs and sign up. We'll soon have corn and oats and barley fields flourishing hereabouts. And the cream of it is, there won't be any Cheyenne Indian problem left around here."

"Sounds too good to be true," said the man. "But I'm all for it. It's a damn shame, that good land going to waste so buffalo can ruin it. The gum'ment had no right to set it aside for the savages."

Hiram's big, bluff face was divided by a grin. "That's my point. Now Mother Nature has come to the aid of the white man. You boys get on out there and stake you out a tomahawk claim. What the paper collars in Washington have given to the red arabs we're taking back for the white man!"

Little Horse soon learned what his friend meant by "flying." And the idea made him nervous.

"We should travel through the trees?" he said doubtfully. "Brother, have you visited the Peyote Soldiers?"

"No peyote dream," his friend assured him. "Look yourself. Between this new camp and the confluence, the trees are thick and close. See how the tops weave together like fingers? Big Tree and Sis-ki-dee will watch by river and ground, but never up into the trees. It will be slow, but we can get right out over the confluence."

Little Horse didn't like it, but offered no more objections. Like most Indians, the Cheyennes climbed trees only to get a good view in new territory. Their main use for trees, besides harvesting nuts, was for the bark—not only to make many things, but as food for their ponies during the winters. But Little Horse agreed they were up against it this time. They had to try something.

Surprisingly, it went much better than either brave anticipated. Many of the trees were massive oaks or birch, with sturdy and plentiful limbs. A bright moon and unclouded sky assisted their trek—especially through the birch trees, for their silver bark reflected well and showed sturdy limbs easily.

There were tense moments. Long jumps between limbs, for one thing. And occasionally they were forced to climb down briefly to reach another good tree. This left them exposed on the ground. But before too long, both of them were creeping out onto a massive limb overlooking the confluence of Salt Lick Creek and the Powder River.

And what they finally discovered there made the journey well worth it.

Wordlessly, hanging above them like bats, the friends watched the paleface work crew working with shovels and graders. They worked in the moonlight, making little noise above the purling of the water. As best as Touch the Sky could guess, they seemed to be reinforcing the new turn in the creek, heaping gravel and dirt on the bank.

However, this seemed minor to Touch the Sky, hardly the kind of work that could alter a huge creek's flow so drastically.

He found out why when he saw a familiar face ease into the moonlight to supervise the work.

Captain Seth Carlson! The two Cheyennes exchanged a long glance.

"How's it going, Meadows?" Touch the Sky heard him say.

"Hunky-dory, Cap'n. That last nitro blast done good work. Thanks to that tunnel, we got the bed sloped perfect now. It won't be nothing to shape things up topside."

"Good man. Work for about another hour tonight, then secure all the tools in the barn."

"Right, sir. You want us to ride back to the fort?"

"No. Colonel Nearhood has got a bug up his ass to visit the rainwater cistern we're supposed to be working on over at Beaver Creek. Take the men and report to the camp there. By the way, have all of you taken your gear out of the barn?"

"Yessir."

"All right. Remember, from now on stay clear

of the barn except when you're storing or getting tools."

"You got it, sir."

Touch the Sky and Little Horse watched the officer speak to a few more men before swinging up onto his cavalry sorrel and riding off.

The barn. Touch the Sky could see it from here, its shake roof looming up from the trees surrounding it. He had paid it little attention. But Carlson's remarks made it clear that structure was somehow important to this infernal project. Important for more than just storing tools.

Thanks to that tunnel. What tunnel?

Whatever that hair-face soldier had meant, the very word "tunnel" immediately jolted Touch the Sky. For it was a tunnel that he and Little Horse had faced in that awful death vision.

Chapter Eight

"I tell you this much, Quohada," Sis-ki-dee told Big Tree. "They are near. You may place my words in your parfleche, for they have substance. They are near."

The two renegades stood in the deep shadows under the canopy of trees that crowded the confluence of Salt Lick Creek and the Powder. Uncle Moon had clawed his way high into the sky. They could see the paleface work crew from here, putting the finishing touches on their mischief.

"They are near," the big Comanche agreed. He had removed his bone breastplate to avoid reflecting moonlight. Both braves wore vermilion to cut reflection from their skin. But this was not a scouting mission, it was a blood hunt, and both were heavily armed.

"Near," Big Tree continued, "but 'near' is not a target when you are eager to close for the kill. How many times has the tall Bear Caller been 'near' us? And how many times has he slipped away like water through a net?"

Big Tree had used the nickname given to Touch the Sky by Pawnees after, they claimed, he'd used magic to summon a grizzly bear to his aid.

"How many times?" Sis-ki-dee said bitterly. "Better to ask how many ways can a man be played for a green-antlered fool? But never forget, Quohada, true it is, he still wears his plew. But so do we wear ours! How many times has he tried to kill *us* and failed? I spent most of one night on that iron horse with him and those Wendigo-spawned white orphans. He searched, and though he got his blade into me, he could not stop me from gutting one of the children."

"No. But he stopped us from ransoming the rest of them. Just as he has stopped us from every scheme that might acquire gold for our new Renegade Nation. Just as he will stop this scheme of the hair-faces if we are not successful this time."

"If we fail this time," Sis-ki-dee said, "then I will finally believe that the tall one is indeed protected by big medicine. Even as we speak, the Wolf Who Hunts Smiling is making their world a hurting place. Hiram Steele and Seth Carlson have made a pact between them to kill Touch the Sky. Have you seen the hatred in their white eyes? By day and night this area crawls with greedy white men eager to earn gold for the tall one's scalp. Every sense tells me they have finally ridden to the Last River."

Both braves fell silent and again listened for any sounds that did not belong to the night. But all seemed well. Only the steady scraping of tools, the hooting of owls, the rhythmic rise and fall of the insect hum that was always loud near water could be heard.

While Wolf Who Hunts Smiling searched the backwaters and adjacent meadows for the enemy's ponies, the two renegades had covered the valley floor. But neither the water nor the game traces nearby had yielded any clues to the intruders' whereabouts.

Either brave could find sign on bare rock. Just as either brave could move with such silence and stealth that he could steal a sleeping woman from her husband's bed without waking either. Yet all their skill and cunning were now as useless as a spavined horse.

"I know they are close," Sis-ki-dee insisted again. "I can smell their Cheyenne stink as clear as bear grease in a Crow woman's hair."

Big Tree was about to reply when something dropped down the back of his neck and lodged between his foxskin quiver and his shoulder.

He reached up and pulled it out. A piece of bark.

Bark? Why?

He showed it to Sis-ki-dee, then pointed up into the trees above them.

Neither brave said a word. Nor were they convinced it meant anything. The bark could easily have been loosened by a nocturnal animal.

But *this* was the spot where their enemies wanted to be. And they were nowhere else around. Why not overhead?

"You must be wrong," Big Tree said loudly, flashing a caution sign to his friend. "There is no sign of them. I say they have gone back to their summer camp to rest and recruit new ponies. We will not see them this night."

At first, intent only on eavesdropping on the work crew, Touch the Sky and Little Horse were not aware that their enemies had wandered under the very tree in which they were hidden.

However, soon the sound of their voices drifted up to them. The sound, but not the precise words.

Touch the Sky's first reaction was one of numb fear. He and Little Horse had been able to carry only their sash knives for this climb. Knives against Sis-ki-dee and Big Tree would be as pathetic as a sisal whip against a raging she-bear.

But then the humor of it occurred to both hidden braves. After all, there was no reason to think even these two expert stalkers would ever decide to search every tree on Maiyun's green earth. If they stayed quiet, they were safe.

Little Horse nudged his friend, thinking the same thing. Hugging a fat limb, both braves enjoyed a brief grin in the darkness.

Speaking very quietly, Touch the Sky said, "Now we know where they are. If we watch where they go when they leave, we will not need to stay in the trees."

Little Horse nodded, anticipating a relatively easy journey back to their cold camp. Like his companion he was sleepy and hungry.

The steady drone of voices rose to identify the speaker: Big Tree.

"There is no sign of them. I say they have gone back to their summer camp to rest and recruit new ponies. We will not see them this night."

Little Horse nudged his friend again. "Thus the great red hunters," he whispered. "Were we any closer, they would be wearing us for war bonnets."

Despite the humor of the moment, Touch the Sky could not help feeling a little nubbin of anger and resentment. For a long time now it had festered within him like a slug festering in pus. Thanks to those two below, every day for him and those foolish enough to love him was like a brutal initiation rite. Other men could lie in peace with their women. But for him and those who followed him, "peace" was an illusion. One created by the Wendigo to drive men mad—as elusive as the fabled white buffalo whose birth would mark the coming epoch of the Red Nations.

But he forced himself to shake off such thoughts. For now they must only be patient and wait for their enemies to leave.

"Yes, Quohada, you speak straight words," Sis-ki-dee said. "We will not spot our fighting Cheyennes this night. They have eluded us yet again."

As both braves appeared to be carrying on a

mundane conversation, a secret plan was going forward. Sis-ki-dee produced two paper cartridges and chewed them open, ramming the double charge of powder down the muzzle of his North & Savage. This was to produce extra muzzle flash.

While he thumbed a primer cap into place behind the hammer, he motioned to Big Tree. The Comanche shrugged his osage-wood bow from his shoulder and pulled a handful of arrows from his quiver, notching one and holding the rest ready in his left hand. Big Tree could string and launch up to twenty arrows in the time it took a soldier to charge his rifle once.

Big Tree understood the plan immediately. In the darkness, a double-charged muzzle flash would produce excellent light. He must stare overhead and hope for a target, saturating the area with arrows. After all, even one brief glimpse would orient him—he had once skewered a Pawnee through the vitals thanks to a flicker of lightning.

"Yes, buck," Sis-ki-dee said, raising his voice as he moved into position. "As you say, his squaw Honey Eater is a fine little tidbit. In a tribe known for beauties she stands out. I mean to top her while the Bear Caller looks on. That is, if he is still alive to witness my prowess as a lover."

Touch the Sky was growing apprehensive.

It had sounded like the two renegades were about to depart. Now he could hear them talking some more.

This time it was Sis-ki-dee's voice that rose in volume. When Touch the Sky heard the usual filth about Honey Eater he frowned deeply— not from anger, for the vile trash spoken by these two had long ago ceased to prick his thick hide.

No. What troubled him was the fact that Sis-ki-dee was speaking the words as if to goad. Did that mean . . . ?

Alarm tingled his nape.

"Brother!" Touch the Sky whispered. "They have—"

KA-WHUMPF!

The double-charged roar of the North & Savage seemed like the loudest noise on earth. The ball whistled harmlessly past them and snapped off a limb. But for an eyeblink's time, Touch the Sky could see every limb and leaf around them in the intense muzzle flash.

Fwip! Fwip! Fwip! Big Tree loosed a mad flurry of fire-hardened arrows at their spot. Luckily the thick limb took most of them, loud thwacks sounding all around them. Touch the Sky felt a burning line of pain as one creased his elbow. Another nicked his heel.

But though they survived that initial volley, their position was known. Even now Sis-ki-dee was ramming another charge home, planning to illuminate them again. And this time Big Tree would be even better oriented to control his shots.

"Brother!" Touch the Sky said. "Nothing else for it! Dive into the river, then stay under the surface and swim hard!"

As loath as his companion was to submerge in that bad-death river, there was indeed nothing else for it. Both braves lowered themselves until they were hanging; then, even as Sis-ki-dee's rifle spat fire again, they plummeted into the channel of the river. The loud splashes announced their move.

"There!" Touch the Sky heard Sis-ki-dee shout. "In the water!"

Arrows sliced into the river all around them, but both braves kicked furiously even as they hugged the bottom. The river was down considerably now, thanks to the paleface treachery. But it was still, thank Maiyun, fairly deep and swift in the middle. Soon they had left the deadly confluence well behind them.

Chests heaving with the exertion, both braves waded ashore and immediately took cover in the thickets.

"Will they follow us?" Little Horse wondered.

"I doubt it," Touch the Sky said. "Big Tree wears two quivers. But he must have emptied both of them by now. Still, this is no place to stand and discuss the causes of the wind. They are too close. Move quick, brother, but attend to your senses. This valley is filled with starving curs, and we are the red meat they crave."

But even as they moved back to the treeline, Touch the Sky was thinking about how they were going to get inside that barn.

Wolf Who Hunts Smiling worked patiently and proficiently in the darkness.

He did not truly expect to find Touch the Sky

and Little Horse, not when they did not wish to be found. Nor was he eager to do so. Closing with either one of those two was a bloody task for ten men. Both together would be a match for a Bluecoat regiment.

But Indians without ponies were soon dead Indians. So far, he had decided, his two tribal enemies had been sneaking around on foot. Soon, however, they would need horses to make their escape.

Good places to hide horses were plentiful in Blackford's Valley. But Wolf Who Hunts Smiling knew they would want their ponies near to hand. Therefore he limited his search, at first, to the best places within a reasonable distance of the confluence.

He also knew a thing those two were not aware he knew. Little Horse had trained his pony to respond to a soft, warbling whistle like a thrush. Hearing it, the little cayuse would immediately come to his master.

Wolf Who Hunts Smiling combed the thickets and copses and hidden meadows, patiently repeating the whistle.

He flinched when he heard the familiar report of Sis-ki-dee's rifle. A wide, lupine grin divided his face. The Blackfoot was a bullet hoarder—if he fired his rifle, it meant he had a sure target. It boomed a second time. One for Little Horse, too?

Again Wolf Who Hunts Smiling made the warbling whistle. And this time a soft nickering responded. Moments later, Little Horse's cayuse and Touch the Sky's paint were greeting him fondly, reassured by the familiar Cheyenne smell.

It was a moment's work to throat-slash both of them. At first, before they buckled on their forelegs, there was an eerie trumpeting sound as air rushed through their gaping throats.

Elation hummed in Wolf Who Hunts Smiling's blood. Sis-ki-dee and Big Tree giving them hurt at the confluence, their ponies dying— Touch the Sky and Little Horse were trapped. They had no place to run, and no way to run there if they did.

"The worm has finally turned, Woman Face!" he announced into the black maw of the night. Then Wolf Who Hunts Smiling disappeared into the darkness.

Chapter Nine

"That's all we goddamn need!" Hiram Steele raged, his face bloating from the intensity of his anger and frustration. "See it? See it, Seth? What did I tell you? It's happening all over a-goddamn-gain!"

"Hiram, for Christ sakes, simmer down—"

"Simmer a cat's tail, you blockhead! You heard what the buck just told us. That red bastard Hanchon *heard* you talking to Meadows. He spied on you. All the men I'm paying, and they still got through."

"If I was you," Carlson warned quietly, eyes sliding to the two renegades beside them, "I'd put a stopper on the 'red bastard' talk, if you catch my drift. These two aren't exactly as sweet as scrubbed angels."

Despite his seething anger, Steele did indeed

catch Carlson's drift. One good look at Sis-ki-dee in broad daylight could humble a man, his eyes were so insane and mocking and clearly on the verge of violence. Big Tree, in turn, was so battle-scarred he put a panther-clawed war horse to shame.

"There," Carlson said. "I'll say this for you, Hiram. You've got a hair-trigger temper, but you calm down quick and start talking sense. Now here's some sense for you. You only *figure* that Hanchon heard me and Meadows. I don't even remember what we said. It might have been nothing."

"It's not so much his hearing you," Hiram conceded. "Hell, we *want* to lure him in the barn now anyway, right? It's just the idea that those red bas—uhh, bucks can slip past all of us at will, no matter what we throw up against them."

Wolf Who Hunts Smiling, too, was present at this meeting. Nearby, some cursory work went forward on the rainwater cistern the soldiers were building near Beaver Creek—their excuse for being in the field these days. Now Wolf Who Hunts Smiling laughed with sharp scorn.

"Let them slip around all they want to. It has cost them their ponies. Besides, why do white men sit upon the ground and wail like women over the past? It is too dead to skin! I do not whine when my last shot misses. I concentrate on killing with the next. My plan to lure them into your tunnel is the best one yet. You must be ready, for they may enter that barn as soon as the night arrives."

The two white men exchanged glances. Though they despised this arrogant, lice-infested savage, he was cunning—and this time he was right.

"We'll be ready," Steele assured him. He sent a high sign to Carlson, and the two white men walked off a few paces.

"Your commanding officer still planning on coming out here?"

Carlson nodded. "Supposed to be an inspection. Mainly, though, he's just grabbing some glory. There's an ink-slinger from the *Register-Gazette* coming out with him. They plan to make a big stirring and to-do over how the Army is making life sweet for the homesteaders. Pure crock."

"It's a pain in the ass," Steele agreed. "But unavoidable. Besides, if I just happen to be passing by, we can get some free promotion for our Pikestown project."

Carlson brightened a little at that prospect.

Steele said, "I contacted a lawyer in Laramie. Spelled out the situation here with the new course of Salt Lick Creek and asked him if I calculated my boundary right. He said it looks jake to him. We're going to Territorial Court, it's already on the docket. This lawyer claims that no Indians yet have won a case in the white man's court. Won't be long, Seth boy, we'll be swimming in gold cartwheels."

Carlson's face registered nothing as he watched Sis-ki-dee and Big Tree hunker in the dirt for a smoke with Wolf Who Hunts Smiling.

"It's not the courts I'm worried about,

Hiram," he finally said. "Seems to me you're hitching the cart before the horse, old son. It's Matt Hanchon we have to kill, and pretty damn quick, or our cake is dough."

"We will kill him," Hiram vowed. "Run Meadows and the rest of the men through the plan one more time. We've got snipers and videttes on him by day, a trap in the tunnel by night. So far Hanchon's clover has been deep. But luck can't last a lifetime unless a man dies young."

Touch the Sky did not mind a sacrifice when the cause was clear and just. But his bitterness upon discovering his throat-slashed pony was increased by the murky nature of this mission.

"They have killed our horses before," he finally said, resigned to the inevitable, "and they will again. We must accept that and deal with the practical question. How do we replace our mounts? True, we must work on foot much. But surely ponies will be crucial at some point, at least to escape."

Little Horse nodded. "Clearly, hiding them will be a problem. But I would breathe easier knowing I had a horse."

"We will have horses," Touch the Sky vowed. "And soon. It must have been the work of our wily Wolf. The renegades were well behind us."

Both braves sat with their backs to a solid stone wall, for they had found a small limestone cave, its entrance hidden by a huge tangle of hawthorn. Their weapons lay to hand beside them.

"Brother," Touch the Sky said carefully, "I

would speak with you. It is about my dream vision."

Even in the dimness of the cave, Little Horse paled noticeably.

"Well?" he demanded with a great show of bravado. "Is there a bone caught in your throat?"

"You could not understand what I heard last night," Touch the Sky said. "Do you know that big lodge near the confluence?"

"The one that sags like an old mule?"

"That one. Yes. We must go inside it. Evidently, our industrious paleface land-grabbers are using it as part of their treachery."

Little Horse shrugged. This was not so bad, after all. True, no Plains Indian liked going into confined places when a fight was brewing, but he had gone into smaller ones.

"And inside that lodge," Touch the Sky continued, "we may well find a tunnel, and it will have to be explored."

He used a crude Cheyenne translation for "tunnel," something like "big worm hole." But Little Horse understood.

"What men have done, men will do," Little Horse said bravely. "Who stood back to back at Buffalo Creek and defeated a score of hiders? *We* did, buck! The kill light was in our eyes, and no man spoke to us of surrender. But only tell me a thing, how do we get into this lodge? Look at us now, forced to hole up like badgers."

"How?" Touch the Sky shrugged. "Ask me where the shadows go. We will find a way even as we make it. First we rest, then we eat. Then we must replace our ponies."

"How? Brother, even if it were safe and the current swift, the Powder would not get us back to camp for at least two sleeps. It would take about that long on foot, too."

Touch the Sky nodded. "As you say. But Beaver Creek is much closer, straight-arrow?"

"Straight-arrow," Little Horse said. "What is there?"

"More talk I overheard. The soldiers are there, building a huge water trap."

Little Horse understood. "And where there are soldiers, there are horses."

"Not the best, surely. Too big, too spoiled, too spirit-broken for good combat mounts. But good enough until we can get to our pony strings back in the common corral."

"And then," Little Horse said causally, "that tunnel?"

"Soon," Touch the Sky agreed, "the tunnel."

Colonel Raymond Nearhood was a career soldier whose distinguished service had mostly been east of the Mississippi in administrative work. He was middling honest, as officers of his day went, his greed tempered by a strong dose of Methodist piety. But he was well past fifty years of age and strongly set in his ways. Rather than learn the million and one things a man needed to learn on the frontier, he counted on his subordinates to make him look good.

Captain Seth Carlson had proven indispensable, if sometimes mysteriously independent. Now the colonel praised him lavishly for the benefit of Cyrus Bergman, a reporter for the *Register-Gazette*.

"Here's the very man right here, Mr. Bergman," the colonel said, introducing the two men. "Captain Carlson not only came up with the idea of a cistern for the local citizens, he did the necessary research to master the engineering. All on his own. This man is a cavalry officer by training, and a crackerjack one, too."

Carlson beamed. "That's an O in the last syllable of my name."

"Yes, Captain, I know your name already," the reporter commented. "Weren't you involved in some kind of scandal under the former C.O.? Something about trying to swindle Northern Cheyennes out of some trade goods?"

Carlson flushed and Colonel Nearhood, who knew none of this, frowned so deeply his silver eyebrows touched.

"Must have been someone else," Carlson muttered. He gave the high sign to Hiram Steele. But Hiram, hearing the reporter's remark, had already withdrawn. This Indian lover was no reporter to talk to about Pikestown.

"When this cistern is completed," Nearhood said hastily, pointing over the huge concave digging, "not only can mother ditches be run off it for irrigation, but it will serve as a stock pond, too."

"Interesting," said Bergman, who did not seem too impressed by the project.

The soldiers working on the project were now dressed in clean fatigue clothes and lined up for inspection. There was a slight commotion from the rope corral where their stock was kept. Carlson glanced in that direction, but saw nothing.

Just a snake, he told himself. Or maybe they'd whiffed a bear. Horses hated the smell of bear.

"Colonel," the reporter said, "what do you think about the situation at Salt Lick Creek?"

"What situation is that, sir?"

"You haven't heard? The creek jumped its bank and now feeds into an old bed that goes south by southwest. The Powder now has no major feeders in this area. It's drastically down."

"Yes, of course," Nearhood said, scowling at Carlson for not telling him this. "I am aware of that situation. What can we say, Mr. Bergman? Man proposes, but God disposes."

He beamed when the reporter jotted that into his pad.

"By the way, Colonel," Bergman added. "Any chance of seeing the Coal Torpedo before I leave?"

"Of course, of course," Nearhood said, injecting great joviality into his tone. The Coal Torpedo was his pride and joy, a magnificent black pacer that had been presented to him by Winfield Scott himself. The horse was valued at a thousand dollars in a land where fifty dollars bought a damned good cow pony.

Carlson, Nearhood, and Bergman headed toward the rope corral, Hiram staying back out of the way.

"The Coal Torpedo is trained to hate the Indian smell," Nearhood boasted. "If an Indian even gets fifty feet downwind of him, he'll attack."

"I'll be damned," Carlson muttered. "The rope on the east side is down. We could have lost some . . ."

He trailed off, a sickening churn deep in his belly reminding him of that commotion he had just seen.

"Where in God's name is my horse?" Nearhood demanded.

"The same place," Carlson answered grimly, "as my sorrel. Look!"

He pointed at a low ridge to their west. Two horses, their riders' single braids flying out behind them, were just disappearing over the ridge.

Chapter Ten

"We must, as one tribe, bring this traitor to justice!" Wolf Who Hunts Smiling fumed. "Every great tribe falls, and falls hard, once there is a loss of manly will to punish tribal lawbreakers."

Wolf Who Hunts Smiling had returned to his summer camp after killing Touch the Sky's and Little Horse's ponies. So far as he knew, they were still stranded afoot—if they were even alive. The net in Blackford's Valley was closing quickly, yes. But Wolf Who Hunts Smiling had seen victory snatched from his very jaws too often before.

Every campaign against Touch the Sky had to be a cunning and brilliant stratagem. Now, when it appeared the tall one and Little Horse could not possibly emerge alive from that valley, was the time to prepare for their death in camp.

No letup, no quarter, until the plains were soaked with the tainted blood of Touch the Sky, who had caused the Council of Forty to strip Wolf Who Hunts Smiling of his coup feathers. He valued nothing so much as his war honors, and many would live to regret that decision.

Medicine Flute stepped forward to toss his views into the hotchpot. The clearing was slowly filling with curious braves, more and more of them wondering why Touch the Sky was still gone from camp.

"When he killed our former war leader," Medicine Flute shouted, referring to Black Elk, "Woman Face put the putrid stink of the murderer on this entire tribe! But it doesn't stop there. Have you seen how he openly defies our councils, and even Chief River of Winds says little or nothing? If another brave behaved thus, he would hang from a pole."

"And now," Wolf Who Hunts Smiling said, taking over, nudging his lackey back, "I have seen him huddling with white men at the place where they have stolen our river! Why, unless somehow he has pitched into their game?"

Not every brave gathered believed all of this. The gleam of ambition in Wolf Who Hunts Smiling's eyes was plain to all but a soft-brain. But unfortunately for Touch the Sky and his dwindling supporters, neither Tangle Hair nor Two Twists were present to control this gathering and defend their leader.

"We have been warned about the Southern

Cheyenne Dog Soldiers," Wolf Who Hunts Smiling said. "But how is *our* tall renegade any less danger than Roman Nose? Roman Nose, at least, was born among us."

"What does it take to remove the blinders from your eyes?" Medicine Flute demanded in a voice that still cracked like an adolescent's. "How far will even the most skeptical among us stretch the notion of coincidence? When Woman Face goes on a hunt with us, we find no buffalo; when Woman Face wanders down to the river early in the morning, our war leader is slain; when Woman Face deals with white traders on 'our behalf,' we end up with smallpox blankets!"

This was well done, thought Wolf Who Hunts Smiling. Tonight Medicine Flute had the gift of speaking. The wily warrior moved back away from the dancing flames of a clan fire, letting his lickspittle weave lies like truth.

"Indeed, red brothers," Medicine Flute called out. "Touch the Sky is far more dangerous than Roman Nose and the Dog Soldiers. And more cowardly. Roman Nose announces his rebel's status openly and boldly! They say he first snapped the common pipe, then he and his followers rode out in open defiance of the Headmen.

"Yet only look at our 'Dog Soldier.' He rides out, claiming only he is mighty enough to 'save' our river. Yet have you seen it? Our river is down more than ever since Touch the Sky left. And our own best Bull Whip trooper has seen

107

him hunkering in the dirt with the Mah-ish-ta-shee-da who pox us!"

This was sophistry at its finest, and several braves muttered their approval.

"Brother," Wolf Who Hunts Smiling said to his pretend shaman in a whisper, "they say I can talk tears out of a dead man. But no tongue is more honeyed this night than yours."

However, an older brave named Trains the Hawk called out, "Medicine Flute!"

"I have ears."

"Yes, but is there a brain between them? Did I just now hear you call Touch the Sky a coward? Touch the Sky, who counted first coup at Tongue River?"

"Touch the Sky, who defeated the sellers of strong water?" shouted someone else.

"Touch the Sky, who got our women back from the Comancheros?" called out another. "A coward? Say what you will about the tall one who arrived among us wearing shoes and letting his feelings show in his face. Say he is a traitor, if you must. Call him a murderer. But call him a coward, and you would speak more sense to call a grizzly a flea."

"Nor would that word be used near Touch the Sky's name," shouted a young Bow String trooper, "if he were with us to hear it."

Medicine Flute bristled. He was about to demand more respect, as shaman-by-right. But Wolf Who Hunts Smiling silenced him with a warning nudge.

"Medicine Flute spoke in the flush of emotion, bucks, as we all do now and again. But

never forget that bravery alone does not pre-
clude treachery. I will concede that Touch the
Sky is one of the best—perhaps *the* best—warrior on the Plains. But the Pawnees who stole
our Medicine Arrows were brave, too! Yet, look
how much suffering it cost this tribe before we
got them back. A good warrior may still be a
pretend Cheyenne!

"This Touch the Sky is a Bluecoat spy. He
lives with us, but serves his beef-eater masters.
He ruts on our women, but carries the paleface
stink. He earns gold every time a red man dies!
The sooner we send him under, the safer all of
us will be!"

Touch the Sky and Little Horse had found it
easier than rolling off a log to lighten the Army
corral by two good horses. And since all good
warriors gave the blade a "Spanish twist" once
it was in, they made it a point to take the horses
of the two highest-ranking soldiers present.

But though it was easy to steal them, they
knew it would be the Wendigo's own work to
move through the valley by daylight on their
new trophies. So rather than risk exposure to
snipers, they immediately broke for the table-
land beyond the valley.

Carlson knew them well enough by now not
to bother sending anyone to chase them. Cheyennes specialized in fighting running battles,
and Bluecoats hated to chase them since it was
impossible to know when the brave fleeing before you might suddenly reverse his pony and
charge.

"Carlson is no coward," Touch the Sky said during their first break to water the lathered mounts. "But it is his nature to humiliate and break a man before he kills him. The clean, quick kill of the true warrior does not satisfy his bloodlust to master a man. Failing that, he prefers the ambush with heavy firepower."

Little Horse nodded, watching the magnificent black pacer drink. Doubt clouded his eyes. This was a pretty horse, and Little Horse did not trust pretty mounts. Also, it was huge, easily seventeen hands, as was Carlson's sorrel. Both Indians were used to sturdy, slightly ungainly-looking animals of only fourteen hands.

"Brother," he said as Touch the Sky pulled himself atop a boulder to study the terrain around this little runoff rill. "I can abide the saddle, but I confess, I get dizzy on top of that huge animal."

"Yes, buck, but admit it, have you ever moved so fast at such an easy pace?"

Little Horse grinned, for it was true. This magnificent beast never broke into a gallop. Yet it matched the sorrel for speed. And so smoothly that a man could crimp a shell without losing a grain of powder.

"See anything?" Little Horse asked.

Touch the Sky shook his head, taking care not to raise his head above the skyline. "No dust puffs. Do you feel pursuit?"

Little Horse knelt and placed three fingertips on the ground. "Nothing."

"Good enough. We will spend the rest of this daylight learning these horses. Face it, we have no time to break them, so we must let them break us. I confess, Carlson has a better horse than he deserves. This one seems to have a good nature—not so spirit-broken as most of the Army mounts."

"This Spanish giant, too," Little Horse admitted, "is good horseflesh. I may keep him for my string."

Touch the Sky dropped back to the ground. He flopped on his belly and took a long, cool drink from the rill. Then, somewhat reluctantly, he stood up again. It had felt good to lie there, and it reminded him how little sleep he had gotten lately.

"When Sister Sun goes to her rest," he decided, "we will search out a place to shelter the horses. Either Tangle Hair or Two Twists sent smoke earlier—you saw it?"

Little Horse, busy peeling pemmican from a roll with his knife, nodded. "The Wolf rode back earlier. Meaning he will not be prowling this night, looking for horses to kill."

"No guarantee," Touch the Sky said, "that Siski-dee or Big Tree will not hunt them out. But we must take the risk. We hide the horses, then we scout that barn."

Little Horse knew this was coming, of course, and only nodded. He said in his usual practical tone of battle preparation, "How do we approach it? Land or river? I take it you will not send us back into the trees?"

"One of us by river," Touch the Sky replied, "the other by foot on land. Both from opposite directions. One man is a smaller target, and by separating we have a better chance that one of us will get a look at that barn. And that is *all* we are doing, at first—a quick look to establish what is in there. It was Arrow Keeper who always told me it is best to look before wading in. This stinks like a trap. That is why we are also going to make a diversion. A good one."

Little Horse perked up a bit at this, for it smacked of good sport. Stealing the white men's best horses had reminded him how much he enjoyed bedeviling his enemies.

"What manner of diversion?" Little Horse asked.

"Have you noticed," Touch the Sky said casually, "the dry patch of Johnson grass in the middle of the valley?"

Little Horse grinned. "Hip-high? A good-sized meadow of it, exposed to the wind?"

Touch the Sky grinned right back. Setting fires as a diversion was a common Indian trick—all the more common because it was so effective. Whites seemed obsessed with rushing to a fire and putting it out, whereas most Indians chose to get out of the way.

"It will probably not draw all of our enemies off," Touch the Sky conceded. "But it will distract them, break their concentration on us. If they are trying to lure us into the barn, perhaps they mean to kill us there. Or perhaps they will spring the trap just outside it.

"But listen now, brother, for we must get it right the first time. Whichever of us reaches that barn first must mark the entrance when he leaves so the other will know it has been entered. Since I have no clan, we will both use your clan notch, agreed?"

Little Horse nodded. Touch the Sky meant the distinctive cut that each clan wore in its feathers.

"Mark it when you leave," Touch the Sky emphasized. Little Horse knew that mark served a second, more urgent function. If it was *not* there, it meant that one of them might be inside—still exploring, trapped, or dead.

"Tonight we get the lay of the place," Touch the Sky said. "Then we make our plan. And may the High Holy Ones ride with us."

Chapter Eleven

"Whatever you do," Carlson warned Meadows, "don't try to engage him in a fight. I know that Indian better than any other white man alive— any who've fought him, anyhow. Lay low and avoid a fight."

Meadows winked at the two other enlisted men with them up in the loft of the old barn.

"Hell," he said in his hillman's twang, "this child didn't join the Army so's he could fight. Ain't no heroes here, Cap'n,'cept for you. Ain't that the straight, Dakota?"

Dakota Jones, operator of the ten-barrel Gatling gun mounted on a bipod behind them, grinned and shrugged. "Cheyennes ain't no tribe to fool with. But ain't none of 'em coming up in this loft, you can take that to the bank."

Carlson nodded. "It'll be a sort of pincers maneuver," he explained. "I know Hanchon. I don't think he'll come up here right off the bat—not if he discovers that tunnel first, which he will."

The officer paused to glance below them into the big, dilapidated old barn. The tunnel opening was plainly exposed behind a huge pile of displaced earth.

"Hanchon *might* throw a quick peek from the ladder into the loft," Carlson mused. "If so, don't risk shooting at him. The gun will be well hidden in a stack of hay, plus it'll likely be dark up here. Only shoot at him if it's absolutely assured you will score hits."

" 'At's right," Meadows said, chuckling. He held up a metal box with a wire trailing from it. The wire was hidden under straw, then routed out of sight in the walls and floor. The box was a galvanic-charger device linked to a series of keg bombs planted near the tunnel.

"Leave him to me," Meadows said. "I push this little plunger, and ka-boom!"

Carlson nodded. "Very little solid earth separates that tunnel from the river flowing over it. Those bombs will bring water sucking into that tunnel. If the explosion doesn't kill him, he'll drown."

"Like routin' a prairie pup out of his hole," Meadows said.

"But do *not*," his platoon leader admonished, "blow that tunnel until you know he's well into it. Don't forget, we've got twenty feet or so of entrance shaft that doesn't run under the river. Give him time. If he goes in, he'll explore it all the way to the main gallery. Give him at least three minutes down there before you hit that charger."

"Sir?" Dakota said. "When you think he'll come?"

"He's come a cropper too many times trying to move around by daylight. Besides, there'll be near a full moon tonight, and Hanchon will know that. It'll be tonight."

"You be here, sir?"

"I'd trade a year's pay if I could be. But I have a staff meeting with Colonel Nearhood. After just losing his prize horse to savages, the Old Man's not exactly in a chipper mood. I'm counting on you men. Do I need to remind you about Hiram's two-thousand-dollar bonus if you kill Hanchon?"

"Oh, sir," Meadows said with mock indignation, "we are not interested in no dirty blood money! Why, sir! We're here to make the West safe for women and children."

"You've got a mouth on you, Meadows," Carlson said. "But you're a good man when the weather turns rough. You two just lay low and keep a tight asshole. You've got the best chance yet of killing Hanchon. You do that, and I guarantee there'll be no more hog and hominy on *your* plates."

Touch the Sky and Little Horse followed their plan. What light remained for that day was spent in learning their new mounts. So far this mission had not required horses. But a good horse was like a good gun. A hundred of them were useless if not instantly to hand when needed, while one was enough if it was available at the right moment.

Then, carefully avoiding vidette riders and those river bluffs where the snipers were stationed, they sneaked back into the valley. They made sure to water the horses well and let them graze a few hours, eliminating the need to tether them close to the river or creek.

Since these horses could not be counted upon to maintain silence, the two Cheyennes reluctantly decided to muzzle them with strips of rawhide. It was a miserable way to treat horses, but they could not afford to lose these mounts.

"Draw a reed," Touch the Sky instructed his friend, holding his right hand out to him. "The shortest one will go by land. He will thus have the task of setting that Johnson grass on fire. The other heads in by water."

Little Horse nodded. He didn't notice a third piece of reed tucked up under Touch the Sky's curled fingers—the shortest piece of all. When Little Horse drew the losing piece, Touch the Sky performed a quick sleight-of-hand.

"I lose," he announced. "You take the river."

Touch the Sky had considered this deception carefully before duping his friend. But clearly, the Cheyenne who went by land would arrive first, even with the delay to start a fire. The river route was almost twice as long.

It was not a question of Little Horse's bravery or competence. Touch the Sky was convinced that Little Horse was the finest warrior in the Cheyenne nation. But Little Horse was all Cheyenne, from birth on, whereas Touch the Sky had been raised among white men. The fear of entering that barn, especially at night, was naturally far stronger for Little Horse—especially since there might also be a tunnel in that barn, a second source of supreme terror for an Indian.

Besides all that, Touch the Sky thought, was the matter of justice. It was hatred of Matthew Hanchon that brought these two white enemies into the Cheyenne homeland like some murderous plague. Yet how many times had Little Horse or Tangle Hair or Two Twists suffered at their hands?

Little Horse did not argue. Gambling was a standard way of settling such questions, and no Indian questioned the outcome of chance.

"Remember," Touch the Sky said. "Just a quick look this night. Then we counsel and make our plan. But just to be safe . . ."

He removed a small piece of charcoal from his possibles bag and marked first his, then Little Horse's face with it. Black, to a Cheyenne, symbolized joy at the death of an enemy.

"I have marked us," Touch the Sky told his friend solemnly. "And the color that is on us is death. We may fall this night, brother. No shame in dying. But if you must fall, land on the bones of an enemy!"

Touch the Sky moved out shortly after sunset, leaving his rifle behind and taking his sash knife and his bow and quiver.

He made good time, mainly because he was reckless and violated much of his training. He moved openly through patches of shimmering moonlight, seldom checked his back-trail, and seldom stopped to listen, feel, and smell.

Once he barely leaped under a bush in time to avoid a vidette. He had a clear shot at the man, and might have dropped him quietly with an arrow. Yet he held back reluctantly. It was bad enough that he violated the Cheyenne way by going out from camp at night. He was sworn, by honor and duty, to restrict all killing to pure self-defense.

He wondered how Little Horse was doing. At least there had been no shots so far. But then Touch the Sky recalled that deadly slingshot master. In this valley, death could sneak up quietly on light paws.

Soon enough the Johnson grass was brushing his thighs and hips. Touch the Sky always carried crumbled bark in his possibles bag for use as kindling. He scooped some out now along with his flint and steel.

He made a little mound from the bark, then tore up some handfuls of grass to lay over it. He struck downward a few times with his steel, sending sparks leaping into the kindling. Soon there was a little orange glow that he carefully blew on until a tiny finger of flame leaped up.

That finger quickly became a long arm. Then, as a stiff breeze picked up, flames began snapping and sparking.

Touch the Sky quickly receded out of the light, resuming his trek.

*   *   *

Little Horse, too, had thrown caution to the wind.

He might have lost the draw, but he had no intention of letting his friend arrive first if he could help it. Despite his great fear of that barn, Little Horse's every instinct urged him to protect Touch the Sky. A warrior fought for many things. But one of the most important reasons was to spare his companions.

For one thing, Touch the Sky was Keeper of the Arrows. He was also the tribe's shaman and, in Little Horse's opinion, the best warrior west of the Great Waters. On top of all that was Arrow Keeper's great vision at Medicine Lake. A vision which told of Touch the Sky's great importance to the survival of the Shaiyena tribe.

So now he did not travel underwater, breathing through a reed while he clung to a slow-moving log. Instead, he swam boldly on the surface, holding onto a log, yes, but kicking hard behind it. In this way he made much better time.

He breathed a little easier after he spotted the burnt-orange glow of a good-sized fire further into the interior of the valley. And just as Touch the Sky had predicted, it drew whites the way magnets drew iron filings—he could hear the vidette riders shouting to each other as they galloped to see what was happening.

Still kicking, Little Horse felt the night-chilled water gliding around him. The log began to bob erratically, warning him that a blockage of some sort lay ahead. He craned his neck and spotted a huge sawyer blocking the channel.

But this could not be. He and Touch the Sky had only recently floated through this spot with no trouble. Sawyers did not form so rapidly . . . not by themselves.

Before he could grasp the true meaning of that thought, Little Horse heard sinister, insane laughter from the nearby bank.

Sis-ki-dee!

Desperately, Little Horse craned his neck again for a look ahead toward that rapidly approaching sawyer—just in time to spot Big Tree, hunched down in the midst of it with a knife in his teeth!

Little Horse had the best ears in his tribe. Above the rush of water, he heard the decisive metallic click when Sis-ki-dee thumbed back his hammer.

There was nothing else for it. Against two other men Little Horse would not hesitate to fight. But *these* two were at least one too many for any man born of woman.

With Sis-ki-dee to his right, Big Tree ahead, and the current pushing at him relentlessly from behind, Little Horse had only one escape route and he took it.

He gave the log a mighty heave forward toward Big Tree even as he tucked and rolled to avoid Sis-ki-dee's shot. Then he scrambled up the opposite bank and into the trees.

There was no chance of his reaching that barn, and Little Horse knew it. He would be lucky to last this night. Now he must go into hiding and only hope the gods would smile on Touch the Sky.

* * *

Touch the Sky had enough weighing on his mind as he approached the looming, shadowy mass of the old barn, but adding fuel to his worry was the precise crack of Sis-ki-dee's rifle, coming from the river.

Little Horse!

Had he, after all, sent his best friend to his death?

But Touch the Sky was too disciplined to reason thus for very long. He was a warrior and so was Little Horse. They knew the rules, and even more important, they knew the odds. Both of them had eluded death too many times not to realize that they were living on Maiyun's grace—what the white men called "borrowed time."

Perhaps, once again, Little Horse had thwarted the Black Warrior called Death. If not, he had died as every warrior prayed he might die, in the middle of dangerous action.

For now, Touch the Sky knew he must shut down all thought, for thought would kill him. Now he must only attend to his survival senses.

It was a relatively easy matter to ensure that no sentinels were in the immediate area. The barn itself, while close to the confluence of creek and river, sat on a small knoll with no trees around it.

He circled it several times, studying it, listening, looking, carefully sniffing the air. With help from Arrow Keeper and Little Horse, he had trained his nose to pick up odors white men seldom thought about: liquor, the stinking liniments they used, the heavy bay rum tonic all soldiers wore after a trip to the post barber.

Nothing lingered outside the barn. Deciding this part was secure, he planned his entrance.

There were two easy ways in—the front and back doors, still intact but standing ajar. But he skipped those and opted for a spot in the middle of the barn where several boards had fallen away, leaving a small entrance between the joists.

He hesitated after crouching in front of the hole. For a long moment he felt it: a cold tingling in his nape, his shaman sense warning him that some manner of danger lay within.

But despite the cold ball of ice in his stomach, he had to go in. He had to see if there was indeed a tunnel entrance in that dark, forboding building. A tunnel, or any clue as to what the hair-faces had done to steal the Powder River's water. The Cheyennes could not begin to fight this thing until they knew more about what they were up against. The effect of the treachery was clear—now he must find the cause.

Touch the Sky briefly touched his medicine pouch, drawing ancestral strength and courage from the badger claws he carried within. Then, gripping a rotting four-by-four, he scuttled under the wall of the big barn.

It was a moment's easy work to get inside, listening as he squatted near the south wall. Somewhere in a back corner an owl hooted, but he heard nothing else. Just the sounds of the nearby water.

Nor could he see anything too threatening in the generous moonwash pouring inside. Most conspicuous was a huge pile of dirt about half-way along the wall.

Touch the Sky's eyes cut to a few wooden rungs that had been nailed into a support beam, making a crude ladder up into a hayloft.

He should secure the top, he realized. But it was more logical to look around down here first. Anyone hiding up there would be bound to make noise coming down. He was safe from surprise attack from up there, so long as he didn't offer a clear target.

Hugging the wall, crawling low on his knees and elbows, he moved cautiously down to the pile of dirt. As he eased around it, he abruptly felt a cold stirring in his stomach.

A tunnel entrance yawned before him, a hungry maw calling out to him to enter if he dared.

After all, he admonished himself, you knew it was here. You heard Carlson mention it. So why this feeling now as if a dead man had risen and asked for a hump steak?

You know perfectly well why, another voice inside him responded. Because you saw this tunnel long before Carlson mentioned it. You saw it in your dream vision.

Death by water.

For a long moment Touch the Sky debated going into the tunnel. But then he recalled his own strict orders to Little Horse. Tonight they would only make sure it existed. Then they would make their plan.

Besides, that tingling was back in his nape. There was a time for plunging recklessly forward, consequences be damned. But this was not that time.

Touch the Sky crawled back outside. Before he left, he slipped around front and made a lopsided V notch about halfway up the door frame—Little Horse's clan notch. If his friend had survived, and if he arrived here, he would know that Touch the Sky had already been inside and left.

For a long moment before he left, Touch the Sky stared up toward that loft. He could have sworn he heard a hoarse whisper from up there. But perhaps, after all, it was only a rat.

Now, it was time to return to the cold camp and see if his best friend in all the world still belonged to the living.

Chapter Twelve

"We're not going to get icy boots," Hiram Steele insisted. "That's what those two blanket-asses are counting on, that we'll start to unstring under the pressure."

"Pressure, my sweet aunt," Carlson scoffed. "All they've done is steal two horses and manage to keep giving us the slip. All right, granted, Colonel Nearhood's pacer was a nice little coup for them. But how many dead and wounded we got this time? Not a one. Considering all that's at stake here for me and you, Hiram, this has been a pretty good showing so far. And the best is yet to come."

"That's what I need to hear," Steele agreed. The two men sat under the fly of Carlson's tent, discussing Meadows's report on the events at the barn. Carlson's unit was camped on a little rise near the cistern project at Beaver Creek.

"Where's the Wolf?" Steele complained, craning his neck to study the camp. "Everybody else is here and waiting on him."

"My scouts said he's close," Carlson replied. "He'll be here by the time we finish our coffee. You just simmer down and remember, don't rile the renegades, any of them. Any one of them would gut his own mother for a chaw."

"Why should I rile them? Hell, how many whites I got on the payroll? None of them has come through either. Only one thing will pull us through this, Seth boy—teamwork. From here on out, we've all got to think like one man, one man bent on one target. We're a team, and if any one of us fails, he drags the whole team into the mud."

Carlson nodded. "The thing last night with Hanchon and the tunnel. He *will* go into that tunnel, Hiram, you know he will. But that bastard is not only savage as a meat axe, he's cunning. Guile and deception come natural to him. He suspected a trap. But eventually, he'll go in."

Steele said, "I hope to hell he does. But we can't assume he will. A mouse that has only one hole is quickly taken. That's why we're having this meeting. This is no time to start praying Hanchon takes the bait at the barn. You've seen how a wolverine attacks: fast, savage, unrelenting, never letting up even for a breath until its prey is stone dead. That's how we're going to be. Every place Hanchon goes, we have to make that a hurting place."

Steele gazed out across the distant mountain

peaks of the Wyoming Territory. His gray eyes were determined, but something else, too. They held hard little points of fear and uncertainty.

"Seth," he said quietly. "How bad do you want Hanchon dead?"

Carlson, his sunburned face half in shadow under the brim of his black cavalry hat, was some time answering this.

"I want that red son cold as a wagon wheel," he finally said. "I want it worse than hell-thirst. I want him so mother-loving bad that I'd gladly die too if I knew I was taking him with me. He came between me and your daughter, you know that. She'd've married me if that cunning son-ofabitch hadn't used his lies and guile on her."

Hiram only nodded, encouraging Carlson in his delusion. Hiram knew far better. His daughter had detested Seth Carlson from the first day, and she would have even without Matthew Hanchon's influence.

"Well, soldier blue, multiply your need to kill him by five, and that's how bad *I* want him. But understand this. This project of ours is far beyond the need for revenge. I've got all my savings invested in our irrigation plan. Plus I've made promises to a lot of men around here. If Hanchon whips us this time, I'll do more than eat crow. I might end up, at my age, a bagline bum."

"My bacon's in the fire too," Carlson reminded him. "So far we've given my men plenty of whiskey. But they also expect a nice ration of the profits once Pikestown is up and running. We short them, it could get nasty. I've had a few men in the past file depositions."

"Teamwork," Steele repeated. Impatiently, he slid his watch from his fob pocket and thumbed back the cover. "Where the *hell* is that goddamn Wolf Who Hunts Smiling?"

"Here he comes," Little Horse said triumphantly. "Just as you said he would, brother."

Touch the Sky, too, watched Wolf Who Hunts Smiling approaching along the old game trace that followed the Powder River toward Blackford's Valley.

"He has come to serve his white masters," Touch the Sky said. "I knew he would ride back to camp briefly to plant more lies about what we are up to. Also, by appearing there now and again, he throws off some suspicion."

"While we," Little Horse said, "by staying gone create the impression of greater treachery."

"As you say." Touch the Sky's jaw tensed as he studied his worst tribal enemy's approach. The only good news lately was the discovery of that tunnel and finding out that Little Horse had survived Sis-ki-dee's attack.

"If he is coming back," Touch the Sky mused out loud, "no doubt there is to be a council of our enemies."

He looked at Little Horse. "Buck, has there been enough sport for you on this mission?"

Little Horse grinned, sensing mischief aplenty. "Sport? None at all. Just target-shooting, with us the targets."

Touch the Sky nodded. "Your thoughts fly

with mine. Our enemies are feeling far too cocky by now. They have made the rules all along. So look to your battle rig! We have plans to make about that barn. But first, we are going to follow our wily Wolf. And then we are going to make life warm at this important council."

"Ulrick?"

"Yo!"

"I want you and the rest of the snipers," Hiram Steele said, "to take up new positions. By now Hanchon has spotted all of you."

"You waste your time," Big Tree said, his voice heavy with contempt. "The Bear Caller will not be taken by a sniper."

"He bleeds, too," Steele said. "I've seen him. Don't matter what the Apaches say about this Geronimo who bullets can't find. Bullets can find Hanchon."

"Only if the marksman can find him first," Sis-ki-dee said. "No one finds the tall one until he wants to be found."

Wolf Who Hunts Smiling, too, joined his fellow renegades in this revolt. "It will not be a paleface who kills him," he insisted. "It will be I, Sis-ki-dee, or Big Tree. These paid killers of yours, they are capable men and good shots. But 'capable' and 'good' are not enough to kill Touch the Sky."

"Get it, Tim?" Baylis Morningstar said to Ulrick, scorn poison-tipping his voice. "It'll need some real by-God men to kill Hanchon. Only these Innuns can get 'er done. The rest of us are still on ma's milk, but they're full-growed and about as rough!"

Hiram angrily started to interrupt this battle-in-progress. But Carlson suddenly stood up.

"I'll be a sonofabitch," he said slowly. "Look!"

He pointed toward a long, tree-covered slope about two hundred yards beyond the cistern. Everyone followed his finger.

"Well, I'll be," Hiram said, for there, grazing peacefully, was Colonel Nearhood's magnificent pacer.

"It's draggin' a lead line," Ulrick said.

"Must've got loose," Carlson said, a wide, ear-to-ear smile dividing his face. He had been in trouble with Nearhood since the Cheyennes had stolen that animal from the C.O. Getting it back would make life easier around the post.

"There's your big bad Indian," Hiram scoffed. "Best goddamn horse he ever put his filthy hands on, and he can't even keep it tied."

However, Wolf Who Hunts Smiling, Big Tree, and Sis-ki-dee had exchanged knowing glances. All three braves discreetly hunkered down. They realized they were about to enjoy a good show.

"I'll ride up and get him," Carlson said. "He's not a spooky animal by nature, but the Indian smell might still have him nerved. You two," he said, nodding at Morningstar and Ulrick, "take up my flanks. He bolts, squeeze him in toward me and I'll try to drop a loop on him."

"All of you, hurry it the hell up," Hiram groused. "I want to get this damned meeting over pronto."

Carlson caught up his new mount, a good coyote dun, and swung up into leather, shaking out a loop. Baylis and Ulrick took up spots to the right and left of him, fanning out perhaps thirty yards. The rest of the men watched with moderate interest, glad for some diversion.

They were perhaps fifty yards from the pacer and closing, when the mild diversion suddenly turned into a Wild West show.

A rifle shot rang out, and Morningstar's horse dropped clean, trapping its rider's leg under him. A flurry of arrows soon protruded from Carlson's dun and Ulrick's claybank, both men barely getting their legs out of the stirrups before their horses went down.

It was over in a matter of seconds. Carlson, dazed, was still trying to fumble his service revolver from its holster when the rapid drumbeat of shod hooves emerged from the trees. His own sorrel came charging out, Touch the Sky and Little Horse riding double.

They both unleashed more stinging arrows as they rode. A man went down screaming, an arrow pushing something pink and glistening through his ribcage. Carlson, too, unleashed a banshee roar of pain as a flint arrow point sliced a big piece of meat away from his left buttock.

Carlson leaped behind his dead horse. But Hanchon and his stout little partner ignored the three white men cowering on the ground. They raced toward the pacer. Hanchon made a magnificent leap, at full gallop, and bounced into the saddle of the surprised horse.

And a few eyeblinks later, the two gutsy Cheyennes were charging the rest of the meeting!

Hiram and most of the snipers and videttes wore side arms. Their rifles were propped against trees nearby, but there was no time to get them.

Hiram shouted something incoherent and dived behind a boulder, jerking his Colt Navy from its big chamois holster. The weapon bucked in his fist as the other men opened fire.

In the heat of this surprise attack, their enemy did just what Touch the Sky hoped they would: They foolishly aimed for the Indians first, instead of their mounts. Had they shot at horses, they might have grounded the riders and then killed them at will.

Nor had the defenders counted on Little Horse's formidable revolving four-barrel flintlock shotgun. It was heavy and unwieldy, and often Little Horse's companions teased him for carrying it. But now, close in like this, it showed its effectiveness.

While Touch the Sky unleashed arrow after arrow, Little Horse revolved and blasted, revolved and blasted, sending out a virtual wall of buckshot. Even as Hiram watched, one of the sniper's faces was reduced to a red smear. Another caught a full load in the abdomen, his vitals bursting out his back in a colorful spray that made Hiram's gorge rise.

Not that the whites did not get off many shots. Bullets nipped at their attackers' ears and flew past with a blowfly drone. But courage kept them sure in the saddle, and moments after it had begun, the attack was over.

The two gutsy Cheyennes were retreating into the scrub pines of the east, leaving behind dead and wounded horses and men.

"Hii-ya!" Touch the Sky taunted them, shrieking the shrill Cheyenne war cry. "Hii-ya, hii-*ya!*"

In a final gesture of supreme contempt, both warriors paused and spun their mounts around, rising in the stirrups to lift their clouts. Hiram Steele and the rest of the white men gathered there knew full well what that gesture meant: *Kiss my red ass, white fools!*

Chapter Thirteen

It was the Indian way to boast after a good raid. When Beaver Creek was well behind them, and no pursuers were in sight, the two Cheyennes halted to rest and water their ponies at a natural sink in the Crying Horse Hills. This was in the midst of Sioux ranges, and thus relatively safe for any Northern Cheyenne, cousins to the Sioux.

"Brother!" Little Horse exclaimed, elation still clear in his face. "I am becoming a traitor to mountain ponies! These 'American' horses performed like seasoned warriors! Carlson's sorrel even took a bullet graze without bolting."

Touch the Sky, too, shared in his friend's exuberance. True it was, they'd faced nearly insurmountable odds in a seemingly impossible task. But, oh, how his blood was singing to finally taste a bit of the pony warrior's life again!

"I did my job," he said frankly. "But this time, Little Horse, it was you and your scattergun who made the grass run red with blood. It was a charge to be sung about in the lodges! A charge to be painted by the elders in the winter-count that is the history of our tribe. Nor was it murder, as these palefaces are trying to do against us. They sent out the first soldier, we only sent out the second. Too bad for them that the second soldier was Little Horse of the Northern Cheyenne!"

Soon, however, bleak reality set in. Still watching their back-trail for dust puffs, Little Horse said, "What next, shaman? We have served notice we are not hair-face playthings. We have found the spot where the whites have. worked Wendigo tricks on Salt Lick Creek. We even know where their worm hole is, as well as the identity of our major enemies. Just now we sent two of their lickspittles across the divide. We have accomplished some work, but left much undone. So what next?"

"Two things," Touch the Sky answered promptly, for he was not one to stand and wring his hands where the road was washed out. "We are going to see Firetop, and through him, Tom Riley. And only then will you and I go back into that worm hole the whites call a tunnel."

Little Horse considered this. "Firetop" was the Cheyenne name for redheaded Corey Robinson, the paleface who had grown up with Touch the Sky when he lived in Bighorn Falls under the name Matthew Hanchon. Firetop had once helped save the Cheyennes from a savage attack by Pawnees. To this day he carried a blue feather that guaranteed safe passage among any tribes friendly to the Cheyennes.

"I am always glad to thump Firetop on the back," Little Horse said. "But you would not pick this time for a friendly smoke. How can Firetop help?"

"His only part in it," Touch the Sky said, "will be to bring Tom Riley back from the soldier town. It is Riley we must talk to, brother. We are up against the white man's devil called engineering and demolitions. Tom knows something about such things."

Tom Riley was a cavalry officer at Fort Bates, and was unquestionably Seth Carlson's chief nemesis there. True, Riley was a "mustanger," a former enlisted man who had not attended West Point, as had Carlson. But Tom's brother Caleb was a successful miner in the Sans Arcs range. Tom had helped him from time to time in such projects as blowing out bluffs to build a spur-line railroad.

Little Horse nodded at the sense of this. If a man wanted to learn how to fish, he did not go to a Paiute in the desert. He went to a mountain Ute who loved trout.

"If we must crawl into that worm hole," Little Horse admitted, "by all means, we must parley with Tom Riley. I will die if I must, shaman, but I hope to someday bounce a son on my knee. I want the best odds at living!"

* * *

"So *that* explains it," Tom Riley said. "I knew that yellow-bellied Carlson had to be up to no good. But he's managed to wangle it so I'm stuck on post these days inventorying every piece of gear that belongs to the Fourth Cavalry. I heard about Salt Lick Creek, of course, from my Indian scouts. But I never figured Carlson and Steele for it. I should have."

The four of them sat around a crude deal table in Corey's split-log cabin: Touch the Sky, Corey Robinson, Captain Tom Riley in fatigue clothes, and Little Horse. From time to time Touch the Sky translated something for Little Horse.

"You didn't actually see any blasts?" Riley asked.

Touch the Sky shook his head. "We heard at least one. It was at night, and sounded muffled. As if perhaps it was underground."

"It was," Riley said with conviction. "I'm no engineer, but I know some sappers and miners and I've helped my brother Caleb with several blasts. What Carlson's men did is called hydraulic angle blasting. It's done to change the grade or slope of riverbeds. They've also probably built up the bed with rocks and gravel, sort of a riprap."

"How the hell can they work *under* a river?" Corey demanded. "I understand the tunnel. But wouldn't the water come rushing into it when they set bombs off?"

"The main tunnel is called the gallery," Tom explained. "You don't detonate explosives in the gallery. You run smaller tunnels, called curtains, off the gallery. That plants the explosive very near the water. Then the curtain is filled back up before the bomb is detonated by galvanic charge. Sounds to me like they're done now. What Touch the Sky probably found was the entrance to the gallery. But why didn't they fill it up, I'm wondering. It's stupid to leave evidence."

"They may still be working down there," Corey suggested.

"That," Touch the Sky said, watching his companion Little Horse even though he spoke English, "is why we have to go into it. If the creek's flow was changed from that gallery, then it's only from the gallery that it can be restored to its original course."

Riley nodded. "There's a bit of good news in all this. As with most things, it should be easier to destroy their work than it was to alter that creek's flow. I can maybe help you with advice and equipment. But no way can I leave the post right now—Carlson's got his toadies on me like dark on night. I can ride south, toward Bighorn Falls, and they ignore me. But if I aim toward Blackford's Valley, Colonel Nearhood will know about it. And I'll be digging four-holers."

Touch the Sky asked, "What do you need from me?"

"Your powers of observation, partner. I've known you to make maps and diagrams in your head that are better than ones on paper. You'll have to *look* at that gallery, look close. Look for tools, gabions—containers for dirt—or explosives. If it's incriminating enough, I'll somehow convince Colonel Nearhood to examine it. We could put Steele and Carlson's necks in the wringer, with a little luck. Nearhood has his faults, including a vast ignorance of Indians and the frontier. But he's a rule-book commander, and he abides by the treaties."

But alter that luck just a hair, Touch the Sky thought, and he and Little Horse would be descending into their graves.

"Meaning," he said, "that if the tunnel is just that—an empty tunnel—it will not be evidence enough that they turned the creek?"

Tom shook his head. " 'Fraid not. Not when it's a white man's word against Indians. We know they did it. But proof is elusive in the white man's courts."

"Yes," Touch the Sky agreed. "We know they did it. So if the proof is lacking, we won't worry about the courts."

"Hell, this ain't so awful goddamn bad," said Dakota Jones, stretching out in the hayloft and lacing his fingers behind his head. "It's boring, but what in the Army ain't? Long as the cap'n keeps bringin' us some chewin's now and then, and makings for a few smokes, hell, it ain't so bad at all."

Meadows nodded. He was seated behind the loft's south window, watching down toward the Powder and Salt Lick Creek.

"Long as you got that gun pointed at the top of the ladder," he said, "we got nothing to worry about. Ain't nobody getting up here through a wall of lead."

The Gatling was well concealed in a mound of straw.

"Two hunnert fifty rounds a minute," Jones bragged. "A damn fly couldn't squeak through."

"You just remember," Meadows cautioned. "Don't shoot the moment you see a feather. Wait until he actually climbs up into the loft. For one thing, it might not be Hanchon that peeks up here. Might be that short pard of his. We won't be able to see real good in the dark."

"Say," Jones said as something occurred to him. "If Hanchon goes into the gallery like Carlson thinks he will, and you push that button, will *we* get caught in the blast?"

Meadows, who knew more about those hidden keg mines, shook his his head. "It'll be like the first circle of Hell down below, chappie. But all we'll get up here is a little shook up."

Jones started to say something else, but Meadows suddenly hushed him by raising one hand. "Shush it, boy!"

He moved closer to the window and looked carefully outside into the late afternoon light.

"What?" Jones demanded, knocking some hay aside to check the action of the Gatling.

"Somebody coming," Meadows told him. "And whoever it is is riding hell-bent for election! Hear them hooves?"

Moments later Meadows whistled out loud.

"Well, lick my left one! It's our Innuns, Dakota! They ain't waitin' for dark. Quick, get down behind that Gatling. Not a peep! All they got to do is go into that tunnel long enough, and

141

I'll blow both their red asses to the happy hunting grounds."

It had been Touch the Sky's suggestion, quickly approved by Little Horse. Why wait until after dark, he had asked, to explore that tunnel? The whites were expecting them to do just that.

Better, Touch the Sky argued, to move now while the hair-faces were still rattled from the lightning raid earlier that morning.

Of course, that presented the problem of snipers and videttes. But for one thing, two of them had been felled by Little Horse's shotgun. And of course, they needed good targets. So the two Cheyennes had simply raced to the barn at a full gallop, never once letting up. They also avoided straight lines, not allowing their enemies to "lead" them with their sights.

Even so, several marksmen had taken shots at them along the way, one shot ripping through Touch the Sky's kit. But finally there it was— the barn, looming up before them.

"We must work quickly, brother," he told Little Horse as they swung down from their purloined mounts. "Take your horse right inside the barn and hobble him after we secure the building. Those snipers have mirrors. They will signal to someone that we have come here. We quickly study the tunnel, and then we leave."

Little Horse's eyes were distant with worry. Touch the Sky's death omen was strong on his mind, as was the Cheyenne fear of enclosed places and death by water.

A quick search of the main floor showed the barn was empty.

"Brother," Little Horse whispered, pointing toward the ladder.

Touch the Sky nodded. He knew Little Horse could not go up there—he had never climbed a ladder in his life, and indeed, only once had he faced a set of stairs.

Touch the Sky tested the first rung. Then, pulse thudding in his temples, he eased up to the level of the loft and peered into it.

Nothing. Just mounds of old straw everywhere. But why, as he gazed around, did he feel sweat break out on his back? Perhaps he should climb up all the way and poke into the straw a little?

He decided that was a good idea. Touch the Sky started to haul himself up into the loft.

"Brother," Little Horse called from below, his voice pitched high with nervousness. "If we are crawling into that worm hole, let us do it now while my courage holds. I would get this over with one way or another."

Touch the Sky abandoned his plan to search the loft and began climbing down again. "Do you have the torch?"

Little Horse, staring toward the dark maw of the tunnel entrance, brandished a short limb wrapped with tow that had been soaked in coal oil at Corey's place.

The two braves exchanged a long look.

"Let us go get ourselves killed," Little Horse said, pumping himself up with bravado to mask a nearly crippling fear. "I have no desire to die in my sleep of old age."

Chapter Fourteen

Every fiber of Touch the Sky's being rebelled against descending into that tunnel.

Questions plagued him. Why, if Steele and Carlson had finished their treacherous work, had it been left here to incriminate them? True, whites could treat Indian rights with impunity here in the Wyoming Territory. But Steele had already lost one battle in court, out in Kansas, when he'd tried to swindle Cherokees. Once burned, twice shy. Common sense told Touch the Sky he should have sealed this tunnel.

Unless it were intended as some kind of trap?

Yet what else was there for it? If he ignored that tunnel, he stood no chance of proving white treachery—or at least, of correcting it on his own.

Besides, as Arrow Keeper had taught him, a

man did not always avoid a thing simply because it frightened him. If all Cheyennes behaved that way, their tribe would have been wiped out long before this.

There was one final persuasion: his dream vision. Despite the warning that came with it, the vision was clearly meant to tell him he must enter that tunnel.

Now, as he sparked his torch with his flint and steel, he looked at his companion's whey-faced fear.

"Brother," Touch the Sky said casually, "I would feel better if one of us stayed on guard up here."

Little Horse knew exactly what his companion was doing.

"Fine," he answered. "Give me the torch. I will go down while you keep watch."

Despite the tension of the moment, Touch the Sky mustered a nervy little grin. "Cheyenne," he said fondly, "you were not born in the woods to be scared by an owl. Stay close to me, but cast plenty of glances back toward this entrance to see if we've been followed in. We are going to move quickly. The longer we are down there, the better our chances of staying down there forever. We need to make a mind picture, then talk to Tom Riley again."

"Don't worry," Little Horse said. "I have no plans to whittle a lance while I'm down there."

Each brave made one last check of his weapons and then started into the tunnel entrance.

It was tall enough that they could walk upright, and perhaps as wide across as a wagon lane. As the tunnel descended from the barn, it sloped gradually until at perhaps fifteen or twenty feet it leveled out again.

This exploration would have been impossible without the long-burning torch. It was as dark as new tar down below. Yellow-orange splashes of light revealed the rammed-earth walls and regularly spaced supports of thick logs.

"This explains all the signs of woodcutting we've seen around here lately," Touch the Sky said grimly.

So far, however, they were disappointed in their search for any incriminating evidence. There was no sign of any excavating tools. As far as the white man's law was concerned, there was no more connection between this tunnel and the new route of Salt Lick Creek than there was between the moon and the color of rainbows.

Fear held both braves by the throat. Constantly, Little Horse searched the receding dimness behind them as they moved forward. They could hear the steady flow of the water, very near by. That reminded them both of that horrible death omen.

Touch the Sky slowly rounded a bend in the tunnel. Suddenly, something scurried across his foot and he shouted out. A moment later, feeling like a woman-hearted fool, he watched a huge black rat race out of the glow of the torch.

Abruptly, the tunnel, which Riley had called a gallery, simply ended. Close examination of the walls did indeed reveal the "curtains" Tom had also mentioned, smaller tunnels that had been run off of this one and then filled back in. Presumably, to insert explosives out into the middle of the creek bed.

But these did not constitute proof either.

"Brother," he said to Little Horse, disappointment seeping into his tone, "we have not found the evidence that might have brought the law into this matter. We will describe what we found to Tom Riley, but I don't see how it can help much."

Little Horse, by now so nervous that sweat glistened on his forehead, said, "Shaman, let us cry about our bad luck later. If there is nothing down here, then why are we? I will not breathe easy until this place is smoke behind us."

"As you say. But we will not rush out of here like prairie dogs being smoked from their hole. We might have missed something we will spot on the way back."

"Do it, Meadows!" Dakota Jones urged in a harsh whisper. "Christ sakes, man, *do* it. Blow 'em damn Innuns to hell!"

Jones still hunched down in the straw behind his Gatling gun. Meadows had crept to the very edge of the loft, the galvanic detonator clutched in his right hand.

"Can't" he answered tersely. "Cap'n said to wait at least three minutes. We got one more minute, then I smoke their red asses."

"Now," Jones urged. "Do it now!"

Stubbornly, Meadows shook his head. "One more minute, chappie. There's two thousand dollars in bright yaller boys hanging on this. We got to do it right. This ain't just some blanket ass that's jumped from the rez. Both of them featherheads are mean as a badger in a barrel. If we bollix this up, our hair'll be hanging off their sashes."

They had just begun their return to the barn when Touch the Sky's sharp eyes noticed it in the flickering light: a tiny gleam of wire, protruding from the dirt wall.

Detonating wire. He might not know how to use it, but he could certainly recognize it.

Working quickly and carefully, he followed it with one finger, pulling it gently out of the dirt behind which it was packed.

"Brother," Little Horse urged, "quickly!"

Touch the Sky ignored his friend, for his exploring fingers had just made contact with something hard and cool. He knocked loose some dirt. Bright yellow letters were exposed:

NGER: HIGH EXPLO

His time in the white man's school saved him, for he knew instantly what those partial words said: DANGER: HIGH EXPLOSIVES!

Left over from the plan to divert the river?

No, whispered an urgent voice at the back of his mind. *Not left over. Planted here to kill you and Little Horse!*

"Out, brother!" he abruptly exclaimed, giving his stout little companion a mighty shove toward the entrance. "Fly like the Wendigo is after you!"

*   *   *

"Now, goddamnit!" Jones urged Meadows. "Katy Christ, Jim, *now!* It's been a minute!"

Meadows grinned and nodded. "Fire in the hole, partner," he said softly, removing the cotter key that kept the detonator points from making contact.

He had placed his thumb on the plunger key and was about to depress it when, all of a sudden, the two Cheyennes burst out of the tunnel, chests heaving.

"Hell and corruption," cursed Meadows, leaping back from the edge of the loft.

Still cursing silently, he watched the braves quickly untie their stolen horses' hobbles and lead them out of the barn. A moment later both soldiers heard the sound of two thousand dollars getting away at a full gallop.

"Aw, damn," Dakota Jones muttered. "Hiram Steele ain't going to like this. He ain't goin' to like it one little bit."

"Sounds like keg mines," Tom Riley said when Touch the Sky had explained their little adventure in the tunnel. "And there's no way they were left there by accident. Carlson has to play hell to get his hands on demolitions. He's not about to leave them behind. They were planted there to kill you, I'd stake my commission on it."

"So how's come they're still alive?" Corey demanded from across the table.

Touch the Sky answered this one. "Because we went in the daylight," he suggested. "And our enemy is looking for us by night."

149

"Could be," Tom agreed. "The main thing is, you made it out."

"With no proof," Touch the Sky said bitterly.

"With no proof," Tom agreed. "But assuming you've got the stones to go back down there, your problems may be over."

Touch the Sky watched his friend closely. "Well, do I have to beg for more?"

Tom's mouth twisted into a grin. "You don't see it? A keg mine—even better, a few of them—delivers one hell of a wallop. Planted where they are, they won't disturb the new grade of the riverbed. But if you and Little Horse were to dig out one of those old curtains, you could stuff the mines in one of them—much closer to the water. You'd need some kind of detonating device, but we could rig that. With luck, you could blow Salt Lick Creek right back into its former route."

Just thinking about going back down in that death hole made Touch the Sky's skin go clammy. But Tom was right. This was a chance—perhaps the only chance—to beat Carlson and Steele at their own game.

"True," Riley added, "Steele and Carlson will get off unpunished. But not really. By now, can you imagine how much work and money they've stuck into this project?"

"Yeah," Corey said. "But, hey? What keeps those two from doing it all over again?"

Tom shook his head. "Can't happen. Nearhood knows now about the creek changing its bed. Even a man like him, with his head stuck up his sitter half the time, would snap wise if the creek jumped back to its old bed and then—wham—jumped out of it *again*. Hell, carrot-top, even you ain't that consarn stupid."

By now Touch the Sky had debated all he needed to.

"Tom's right," he said. "It's the only hope. And the longer we wait, the less our chance of blowing that tunnel before they fill it back in."

"I can tell you how to detonate those mines," Tom said. "And I can probably manage to get you some blasting fuse. A remote detonator would be best, but I can't lay hands on one. It's risky, Touch the Sky, I won't kid you."

Touch the Sky nodded but said nothing. He was well aware of the risk—and well aware that he still had to translate all of this for Little Horse. That stout warrior had been so happy to get out of that tunnel that he had scattered his white man's tobacco—the tobacco he wrangled from Touch the Sky—to the winds as a thank-you to the holy ones. How would he take it when he learned they were going back down that "worm hole"?

But what was the alternative? To let Hiram Steele and Seth Carlson not only dry up their most important river, but steal their best Cheyenne hunting ranges as well?

"Start talking, soldier blue," Touch the Sky told Riley.

Dakota Jones had been wrong. Hiram Steele was surprisingly philosophical about the bad news from the barn.

"Never mind, Seth boy," Steele told Carlson

as they sat in the soldier's bell tent, sipping good rye whiskey. "Just never mind. It's like you said yesterday. We haven't killed Hanchon this time either. But here's the difference. That red son-ofabitch has failed to stop us, for once! *Let* the bastard live! Actually, that's even better. Now he'll have to bear witness while his 'proud and noble people' starve and go naked!"

Carlson's glum face slowly settled in a smile. "By God, Hiram, you're right. We've been so obsessed with killing Hanchon we haven't considered any alternatives. Once their buffalo ranges are plowed under with barley and oats and corn, the Cheyenne will be reduced to begging and growing gardens. Just like the Poncas, the tribe they're always scorning as dirt-scatterers."

Hiram nodded. "Then it's settled. Have a work crew fill that tunnel in as soon as possible. Pard, we got an irrigation project to get started on."

Carlson grinned. "You know, Hiram? In a way, we succeeded after all. For a man as proud as Matthew Hanchon, watching his people go under *will* kill him."

Chapter Fifteen

"I always wanted a long life," Sharp Nosed Woman said sadly. "Even with all the grief this tribe has faced, I wanted to live a long time and see the little ones dance the Animal Dance as I did in my youth. But *this* makes me wish I had died a-borning, rather than live to see it."

Honey Eater's aunt, not one to cry at trifles, now turned suddenly from the rest to hide the crystal teardrops spilling over her lashes.

"Our Powder River!" she cried. "Well over forty winters now have I returned here with the rest of my people. I have felt the lush new grass under my bare feet, smelled the clean, sweet smell of prairie and river. Down there, Honey Eater, around that little cottonwood island at the turn, that is where your bride lodge was built! Oh, how the young girls sang your love when you and Touch the Sky exchanged the squaw-taking vows."

Honey Eater, busy helping her aunt fashion a travois from sapling poles and buffalo-hair ropes, was near tears herself.

Watching them vigilantly from opposite flanks were Tangle Hair and Two Twists. Now Honey Eater held Tangle Hair's eyes as she replied.

"*You* remember my bride lodge, Aunt? Good. Then how must it reign in my mind? Never will I forget the words of this one here"—she pointed at the shy Tangle Hair—"as we were about to enter. He told Touch the Sky, 'We made the entrance tall, brother, because we knew you would be passing through it. And none taller than the woman on your arm.'"

Tangle Hair flushed and looked across the dwindling river, trying to hold his face passive as warriors must. He loved Honey Eater like the sister he'd never had, but it would not do to show womanly feelings.

"He said that?" Sharp Nosed Woman exclaimed, new tears springing to her eyes. "Our Tangle Hair is a poet, and a fine one."

Two Twists secretly agreed that Tangle Hair, a stout warrior indeed, was also a man whose well of inner feeling was deep—and he admired him greatly for this. Nonetheless, he could not resist teasing him a bit.

"Oh, Tangle Hair," he called out, "yesterday I saw a hawk kill a mouse. Please sing the mouse's eulogy in phrases that will make my eyes leak!"

"You beast," Sharp Nosed Woman said, though with no real rancor, for she considered Two Twists one of the tribe's best young men— if a bit mouthy.

All this levity, however, could not erase the horrible reality now pressing on Honey Eater: Because of the disappearing river, they were packing up their camp and moving to a new summer camp.

River! That was like calling a burial mound a mountain. Just look at it. The only thing left now was a narrow, sluggish channel surrounded by scabrous, drying mud.

She, too, had known no summer camp but this one. Despite all they had suffered here— pestilence, raids, near-starvation—this was her home. And it was the tribe's ancestral home. The Powder River for summer camps, the Tongue River for winter camps. Since the days when the Shaiyena were driven from the woodlands now called Minnesota, that had been the pattern.

But tragic as it was to be forced to move, that was not the end of her troubles. For understandable reasons, notably Touch the Sky's long, unexplained absence from camp, the collective anger of the tribe had focused on her.

Little Bear was playing nearby, weaving a necklace of flower stems. She watched her son for a few moments, enjoying his blessed innocence. Oh, sacred Maiyun, what trouble was destined for that little mite once he wore a warrior's shield! But for now, so far anyway, his was a world in which he was loved and cared for and secure.

Now what was in store for him? Especially with the tribe's anger focused on his mother and father?

"You three," she suddenly said to her aunt and their two guardians. "You do well at pretending I am not the outcast of this tribe. But for your own safety, perhaps you had better spend less time around me."

Honey Eater was not being overly dramatic. She had indeed become an outcast. No one in her clan would touch a utensil she had touched. Though of course no Cheyenne, even a murderer, was ever starved by the tribe, her meat rations were always piled separately during the hunt distribution.

"And perhaps *you* had best control your tongue before I box your ears," her aunt said sharply. "We three know where your man is. He is out risking his scalp to solve the mystery of this disappearing river. As for those two"—she nodded toward Tangle Hair and Two Twists—"they have no ears for such talk."

"Indeed, sister," Two Twists said, "you are perhaps a new outcast. But Tangle Hair here and I have been taboo since we crossed our lances with that of Touch the Sky. Where would we go if we didn't guard you? They don't want us."

"Never mind," Two Twists added. "Arrow Keeper said once that if one man knows better than the Council of Forty, that man is a majority of one. Touch the Sky, too, is a majority of one. And count upon it, the majority *will* rule."

"Hii-ya!" Little Bear suddenly shrilled, imitating the war cry. Hearing it, Two Twists and Tangle Hair both grinned proudly.

Honey Eater and Sharp Nosed Woman, however, exchanged long, sad glances. Glances women understood and men never noticed.

"Best face it like men," Touch the Sky told Corey, after saying the same thing to Little Horse in Cheyenne. "There's a good chance that whoever sets up the blast will get killed before it's ready. That means, since Corey will be on sentry duty outside the barn, Little Horse will have to know the procedure too."

The three friends had decided on a dawn raid, a straight ride from the rim of Blackford's Valley to the barn and the confluence. By choosing dawn, they had covered their ride through the valley in darkness, yet arrived with enough light to scout the barn.

Corey had insisted on coming along this time. Though Touch the Sky was deeply reluctant to risk his friend, he admitted he desperately needed the help. Corey, a fair to middling hand with his sixteen-shot Henry, was to dig a rifle pit in good cover within range of the barn.

Now all three hunkered behind some blackberry brambles while Touch the Sky laid a coil of fuse and a cylindrical metal object in the grass.

"I saw more than one mine," Touch the Sky said. "I'm not sure how many. But all of them should be shoved into the curtain just to be sure we get the job done. Only one mine needs to be wired—the others will go off if they're close enough."

"These little worm holes you call curtains," Little Horse said. "They are full of dirt."

"Loose dirt," Touch the Sky said. He nodded to a spade protruding from the boot of Corey's saddle. "Tom says it will come out fast and easy. This hard thing is a blasting cap. You crimp the fuse to it like this. Then the blasting cap is inserted into a hole—Tom called it a cap well—on top of the mines. Do you have the sulfur matches Corey gave us?"

Little Horse nodded, feeling in his parfleche to make sure.

"Ready?" he said in Cheyenne to Little Horse. His friend nodded.

"Ready?" he said to Corey.

"Hell, no," Corey said. "You boys're the big warriors. Me, I'm just a humble carpenter. But yeah, let's go. Hiram Steele once sent that bastard Abbot Fontaine to play thump-thump on me. You remember?"

Touch the Sky nodded. "How could I forget? Your face was bruised so purple it looked like a bunch of grapes."

Corey grinned. "Yeah, but it don't matter. Cuz ol' Little Horse done for Abbot's butt. Done for him good."

"Tether our horses here," Touch the Sky decided. "We can get to the barn on foot in maybe ten minutes. That way we can listen better as we approach."

His decision turned out to be crucial. The

stealthy trio were about to break out of the last line of trees when they heard the snuffling of horses and the chinking of bit rings.

Touch the Sky threw up a quick hand, halting his companions. He moved forward a few paces, knelt, and cleared some brush with one hand.

A paleface work crew was assembling just outside the barn—a work crew equipped with shovels and wheelbarrows! A crew obviously intending to fill in that tunnel.

The cold bile of fear erupted up Touch the Sky's throat. He motioned for his friends to come forward and join him. He wanted them to see it too. The palefaces were about to seal off the Cheyennes' only chance to revive their river and save their homeland.

The sturdy Little Horse, a stranger to panic, could not keep his eyes from bulging like wet, white marbles.

"Brother," he whispered. "There are three of us and at least fifteen of them. They all have carbines. I am willing to risk it. But do we ask Firetop to face these odds? This is not his homeland stand, but ours."

"As you say," Touch the Sky agreed. "Therefore we even the odds. Look, coming out the door of the barn."

Little Horse did look. A soldier lugging a huge gun with legs on it was emerging into the new dawn light. He set the gun down outside the door and wiped the straw off his uniform.

"A Gatling," Touch the Sky whispered. "I know the gun. Tom showed me how to fire it up

159

in the Sans Arcs. Is your shotgun loaded—all four barrels?"

"Is a Comanche as ugly as a buzzard?"

"Good. I have a plan. A plan more crazy than brave. Corey stays here, potshotting as many as he can. You slip over to their right and rain pellets on them with the scattergun. As soon as all four loads are spent, switch to your bow. But first target of all—kill that hair-face who carried the gun out and is still standing beside it. I am taking over that gun, and I mean to sweep these locusts back."

It was a crazy plan indeed, Little Horse saw, likely to kill both of them, and thus, already his blood was up for the challenge.

Touch the Sky translated for Corey. "You will be critical once Little Horse and I go inside the barn," Touch the Sky assured him. "I'm going to drive them back for a while with the Gatling. But they'll get their courage back after we go inside. It's up to you to discourage them. But stay covered. I'm used to looking at your ugly face."

"Well, yours still scares hell out of me every time I see it," Corey assured him, masking his fear. "Now quit the damned speechifying, and let's make some crooked soldiers earn their pay for a change."

Corey moved slightly to one side and quickly dug out a wallow, using one half of his bull's-eye canteen. Touch the Sky waited until he had shells ready to hand and had dug his sighting elbow in good.

"Now, brother," he whispered to Little Horse.

"Move quick but quiet. See that wide oak over there? Get behind it, then open fire. At the first shotgun blast, I take off for the Gatling."

"Brother?" Little Horse said, hesitating.

"What, buck? Time is wasting."

Little Horse grinned. "Good chance you'll be killed. If so, may I have the licorice drops you have been hoarding in your legging sash?"

"Why not?" Touch the Sky said, grinning back. "After all, I stole them from your parfleche."

He slapped his friend hard on the rump, and Little Horse took off at a crouch. He leapfrogged from tree to bush, easily evading the whites in the grainy half-light. They were busy breaking out their tools and getting torches ready.

Touch the Sky waited until Little Horse was in position. Then he glanced back over his shoulder to make eye contact with Corey.

The redhead nodded.

Touch the Sky touched his medicine pouch and said a brief battle prayer. Then, every muscle tensed to spring, he gave the nod to Little Horse.

Chapter Sixteen

Tim Ulrick was up before dawn, and heard the noise when a trio of horses headed toward the confluence. He imitated the sound of a loon, and soon Baylis Morningstar joined him at Ulrick's new camp closer to the river.

"I heard it," Morningstar informed him even before Ulrick could ask. "That was the sound of money, Tim."

"One thousand apiece," Ulrick suggested, "if we was to team up on him. I see now it'll take two with *that* one."

Morningstar's hip pouch bulged with steel balls for his powerful sling. He considered Ulrick's suggestion, and decided the man was right. Baylis had never had more than thirty dollars at once in his whole damn life. One thousand, two thousand . . . down in Old Mexico a man could buy a town for one thousand, and all the women in it, too.

"It's a deal, pard," the half-breed agreed. "Now catch up your horse. If we mean to kill those two Cheyennes, we best get it done fast. There's others in line."

All three renegades spotted it just as dawn painted the eastern horizon in copper flames. It was clearly visible in the sky over a distant mountain peak, almost aflame as the new sun backlit it.

For a long time Wolf Who Hunts Smiling, Sis-ki-dee, and Big Tree stared at it in absolute silence. All three were painted for battle, their war kits readied.

Below the spot they occupied on a limestone ridge, Morningstar and Ulrick raced by, heading toward the confluence. Sis-ki-dee looked at them. Then, again, he stared at the object floating in the sky over that distant mountain.

"Big Tree," Sis-ki-dee remarked casually. "I have been considering a thing. I think it is time to visit our men on Wendigo Mountain before they drink our cache of good liquor. I left Scalp Cane in charge, but you know how he can be his own man."

Slowly Big Tree nodded. "As you say. I have new horses to break, too. How about you, buck?" Big Tree added, quartering his horse around to look at Wolf Who Hunts Smiling.

At first, looking at that cloud formation with the others, Wolf Who Hunts Smiling had felt a bitter anger and disappointment. But there were some men whom bees refused to sting, and this Wolf was one of them. He shook off his disappointment, for determination had ousted it.

"What about me?" he responded. "I am with my renegade brothers! White men may charge in to a certain death, but we three are of one mind: Fight only when we can win! *That*"—he pointed toward the horizon—"tells us our part in the fight is over for now, if we are wise. But mark me. Though this is not the time, a time is indeed coming—a time when we three will dance in his guts and smear our bodies with his blood!"

All three Indians crossed their lances as one. And as one, they took a final awed glance at that remarkable cloud over the mountain: a cloud shaped precisely like an arrowhead, the mark of the warrior, the mark visible in Touch the Sky's hair when it was wet and plastered back.

Wolf Who Hunts Smiling thought of something. "Carlson is at the fort, but do we warn Steele? He is with the soldier work crew."

"Would he warn you?" Big Tree shot back.

All three shared a grin, then headed out of Blackford's Valley.

Little Horse had taken up his position behind the oak and was just starting to slip his finger inside the trigger guard. Abruptly, the rapid drumbeat of approaching hooves from behind warned him.

He spun around just as Ulrick and Mornings-tar rounded a turn. Little Horse cursed at having to waste one of four valuable shots, but there was no alternative. Aiming carefully between the two riders, turning the choke to spray wide, he squeezed off a load of buckshot and blew both men from their saddles.

That first blast was still reverberating over the river when Touch the Sky burst toward the soldier lugging the Gatling. A trooper aimed his carbine at Touch the Sky and, behind the Cheyenne, Corey's Henry barked. There was a loud thwap as the slug punched into the soldier's breastbone, evoking a spray of blood and a scream of agony as he collapsed.

Little Horse, meantime, braved almost certain death as he dashed forward. He had to make sure he was close enough to kill the soldier with the Gatling, yet avoid damaging the gun.

Touch the Sky raced in from the south, Little Horse from the north, and their only allies were surprise and Corey Robinson's busy Henry. Little Horse's scattergun exploded again, Dakota Jones slammed back into the wall of the barn, and within moments Touch the Sky was frantically re-attaching the hopper full of shells, which had fallen off when the trooper dropped the gun.

Little Horse used his remaining two shells to good advantage, forcing the frightened soldiers to take cover while Touch the Sky readied the Gatling.

But when Little Horse's hammer clicked uselessly, Hiram Steele was up and charging with a roar like a bull.

"Now, boys!" he screamed. "Now, kill them! The shotgun is spent! Now! Now, do it, goddamnit, *do* it!"

Hiram was so agitated that he was pulling his own shots wildly, the slugs taking chunks out of the barn behind Touch the Sky. But some of the soldiers, already in a prone position, were starting to draw a better bead on him.

"No hurry, brother," Little Horse said with feigned boredom even as the bullets flew past his ears like angry hornets. "These are only white men."

Now Hiram was dangerously close, and Little Horse took the risk of pulling his sash knife and rising to his knees, ready to throw.

"Down, fool!" Touch the Sky ordered, knocking his friend aside with one hand. A moment later the Gatling gun was bucking on its bipod, barrels clicking with precision as Touch the Sky revolved the crank.

A line of snake holes was stitched across Steele's thighs and he cried out in agony, collapsing in the grass. Behind him, several soldiers dropped like sacks of grain before the rest bolted and ran for the woods behind them.

"Hurry, you two!" Corey screamed from his rifle pit. "Hurry! Get in there and blow that goddamn tunnel! The soldiers will be back when they regroup. I'll hold the line as long as I can. But you two better damn hurry!"

Little Horse scrambled to his feet as Touch the Sky pulled the coil of fuse and the blasting cap from his parfleche. They exchanged one final look, and Touch the Sky knew his friend was thinking of the same thing he was: an omen of bad death—bad death by water.

Touch the Sky found a total of three keg mines buried in the wall of the main gallery. If there were more, he didn't worry about them. Tom said three would do it.

While Touch the Sky dug the mines out, Little Horse frantically went to work with the spade, clearing out one of the curtains or smaller side tunnels. These ran close to the water, but stopped a few feet short. Close enough, both Indians hoped, that one good blast would undo the paleface treachery.

Each keg mine was awkward to carry and perhaps as heavy as a small man. Touch the Sky wrestled them down, then helped Little Horse in the frantic effort to clear a side tunnel.

Faintly, they heard shots above them.

"Soldiers coming back," Touch the Sky said grimly. "Hold on, Corey, hold on!"

"Firetop will hold or die in the attempt," Little Horse said, even as the two friends wrestled the first mine into the tunnel.

It would have been a hard job for big men who were well rested. It was agony for these sleep-starved, exhausted warriors. Especially confined in such a small place with enemies somewhere behind them, liable to come down at any moment.

"Take this," Touch the Sky said, gasping for breath. He handed the coil of fuse to Little Horse. "Wind it out toward the gallery. I am going to rig the cap."

Little Horse was more than happy to head

back. Sweat pouring from him, every limb trembling from the cramp and effort, he began squirming back.

Touch the Sky, willing his fingers steady, crimped one end of the fuse to the blasting cap. It contained enough black powder to explode the mines, once inserted into the vertical wells on top.

When all was ready, Touch the Sky joined his friend in flight from the curtain. Little Horse had already snapped off the fuse right where it emerged into the gallery. That should give them plenty of time to get back above ground before the explosion.

Touch the Sky removed a sulfur match and scratched it on the rough sole of his elkskin moccasin. The fuse sparked to life. But shots continued to sound outside, and they knew this battle was far from over.

A moment later, however, and they heard a very welcome sound: Corey's shout of triumph as the Gatling barked into action again. He had made a dash for the gun and now commanded the entire front of the barn! Within moments the sound of opposing guns was silenced.

Both braves whooped in triumph. Just before they broke for the sloping tunnel that led above ground, Touch the Sky made one final check of the fuse.

Even as he glanced down the narrow tunnel, a big clot of loose dirt plopped down onto the fuse, snuffing it out about fifteen feet from the keg mines.

His heart leaped into his throat. Little Horse

saw it, too. He was about to leap into the tunnel when Touch the Sky reluctantly applied one of his white man's skills. He threw a hard upper-cut and knocked his friend partially unconscious.

Corey couldn't hold out forever. Touch the Sky scrambled madly into the tunnel. He found the fuse, pulled it out of the dirt, and somehow got it lit again. Once he was sure it was burning, he began the mad scramble to safety. But he would never make it, never—

"Little Horse!" he screamed, for he could see his friend waiting for him now, guarding the entrance with knife in hand. "Get out! Get out! Now!"

His friend ignored him. Touch the Sky was squirming to get out of the last few feet of the tunnel when strong hands gripped him, tugging. Little Horse had almost pulled him free when the world suddenly came apart.

Never, as each brave was picked up and heaved like so much river-tossed wreckage, had they heard anything so loud. First came a powerful concussion like a mule kick to the skull. Then a huge wall of dirt, followed by a welling juggernaut of water.

It washed over them, tumbling them, heaving, bouncing, and there was no way to get out from under it. The dirt and the water formed instant mud, tons of it, and they were wildly scrambling to get clear of it.

Sticky clay filled their ears and noses and throats, blinded them, held their limbs like tight ropes. Still they struggled, fought, squirmed toward the safety above ground. Fighting thus for their own lives, they could not see how the main brunt of the powerful explosion was churning a huge spray of rocks and water out over the confluence, altering it.

Touch the Sky, choking so bad he couldn't even sing his death song, suddenly felt something slap his face. He grasped for it and felt a rope! He clung desperately with one hand, the other searching the river of mud for Little Horse. He found a wrist and clung to it.

Corey, his face white as moonstone, was just outside the barn with one of the saddled soldier mounts. Expertly, he dallied the rope around the saddlehorn and whacked the horse on the rump hard. It surged forward, and Corey watched two Indians—so covered with mud you couldn't tell them apart if you were their mother—come oozing out of the flowing muck.

"Still not full, but it is rising," Honey Eater said happily almost one full moon after the battle in Blackford's Valley. "And rising well. Soon, we will have our river back. The Council of Forty has ceased all talk of moving to a new camp."

Touch the Sky nodded. He sat with his woman on the rolling bank of the Powder. Little Bear was actually swimming now, in short bursts, showing off for his proud parents.

The tall warrior had learned by now to take happiness like he took food and sleep, in broken doses, snatched when he could. He felt the joy of this moment all the more keenly because of the trouble he knew was coming—was always coming, for the red man.

Hiram Steele, he'd heard, was bitter and ruined, nothing but a common drunk picking barroom fights in Register Cliffs. But Steele was like the red-speckled cough or the yellow vomit that wiped out tribes: a parasite that would always return when least expected, bent on the destruction of the red man.

Yes, trouble clouds were blowing close. But for now Touch the Sky threw back his head and tasted the great love for his woman and child, for this time with them and the beauty of Mother Earth.

CHEYENNE

JUDD COLE

Don't miss the adventures of Touch the Sky, as he searches for a world he can call his own.

Cheyenne #14: Death Camp. When his tribe is threatened by an outbreak of deadly disease, Touch the Sky must race against time and murderous foes. But soon, he realizes he must either forsake his heritage and trust white man's medicine—or prove his loyalty even as he watches his people die.

_3800-5 $3.99 US/$4.99 CAN

Cheyenne #15: Renegade Nation. When Touch the Sky's enemies join forces against all his people—both Indian and white—they test his warrior and shaman skills to the limit. If the fearless brave isn't strong enough, he will be powerless to stop the utter annihilation of the two worlds he loves.

_3891-9 $3.99 US/$4.99 CAN

CHEYENNE

JUDD COLE

Cheyenne #20: Renegade Siege. Born the son of a great chieftain, Touch the Sky was raised by frontier settlers. Though he returned to his father's people to protect his tribe, he knows that without his help many of his white friends will be slaughtered like sheep. For Touch the Sky's blood enemies have surrounded the pioneer mining camp with renegade braves and are preparing to sweep down on it like a killing wind. If the mighty shaman cannot hold off the murderous attack, the settlers will be wiped out...and Touch the Sky's own camp will be next!

_4123-5 $3.99 US/$4.99 CAN

Cheyenne #19: Bloody Bones Canyon. Born the son of a great chieftain, raised by frontier settlers, Touch the Sky returned to protect his tribe. Only he can defend them from the renegades that threaten to take over the camp. But when his people need him most, the mighty warrior is forced by Cheyenne law to leave them to avenge a crime that defies all belief—the brutal slaughter of their beloved peace chief, Gray Thunder. Even Touch the Sky cannot fight two battles at once, and without his powerful magic his people will be doomed.

_4077-8 $3.99 US/$4.99 CAN

Dorchester Publishing Co., Inc.
65 Commerce Road
Stamford, CT 06902

Please add $1.75 for shipping and handling for the first book and $.50 for each book thereafter. NY, NYC, PA and CT residents, please add appropriate sales tax. No cash, stamps, or C.O.D.s. All orders shipped within 6 weeks via postal service book rate. Canadian orders require $2.00 extra postage and must be paid in U.S. dollars through a U.S. banking facility.

Name _____

Address _____

City _____ State _____ Zip _____

I have enclosed $_____ in payment for the checked book(s). Payment <u>must</u> accompany all orders.☐ Please send a free catalog.

CHEYENNE
JUDD COLE

Born Indian, raised white, he swore he'd die a free man.

#10: Buffalo Hiders. When white hunters appear with powerful Hawken rifles to slaughter the mighty buffalo, Touch the Sky swears to protect the animals. Trouble is, Cheyenne lands are about to be invaded by two hundred mountain men and Indian killers bent on wiping out the remaining buffalo. Touch the Sky thinks it will be a fair fight, until he discovers the hiders have an ally—the U.S. Cavalry.
_3623-1 $3.99 US/$4.99 CAN

#11: Spirit Path. Trained as a shaman, Touch the Sky uses strong magic time and again to save the tribe. Still, the warrior is feared and distrusted as a spy for the white men who raised him. Then a rival accuses Touch the Sky of bad medicine, and if he can't prove the claim false, he'll come to a brutal end—and the Cheyenne will face utter destruction.
_3656-8 $3.99 US/$4.99 CAN

#12: Mankiller. A mighty warrior, Touch the Sky can outlast any enemy. Yet a brave named Mankiller proves a challenge like none other. The fierce Cherokee is determined to count coup on Touch the Sky—then send him to the spirit world with a tomahawk through his heart.
_3698-3 $3.99 US/$4.99 CAN

Dorchester Publishing Co., Inc.
65 Commerce Road
Stamford, CT 06902

Please add $1.75 for shipping and handling for the first book and $.50 for each book thereafter. NY, NYC, PA and CT residents, please add appropriate sales tax. No cash, stamps, or C.O.D.s. All orders shipped within 6 weeks via postal service book rate. Canadian orders require $2.00 extra postage and must be paid in U.S. dollars through a U.S. banking facility.

Name _____

Address _____

City _____ State _____ Zip _____

I have enclosed $_____in payment for the checked book(s). Payment <u>must</u> accompany all orders.☐ Please send a free catalog.